Hold Autumn in Your Hand

Hold Autumn in Your Hand

George Sessions Perry

Afterword by
Maxine C. Hairston

A Zia Book

UNIVERSITY OF NEW MEXICO PRESS
Albuquerque

For Claire

I

THE Texas January day was all blue and gold and barely crisp. Only the absence of leaves and sap, the presence of straggling bands of awkward crows, the gray-yellow flutter of field larks, and the broad, matter-of-fact hibernation of the earth said it was winter as Sam Tucker walked along the road, his long legs functioning automatically, farmerly. His body had about it the look of country dogs at the end of winter, when they are all ribs and leg muscles and jaw muscles and teeth. His eyes were bright and dark and small, with no more evil or softness in them than a hawk's. His hands were knotty with big knuckles and were gloved with protective calluses.

A cock quail came out of the burdock hedge at the side of the road just ahead and looked at Sam with a strange, casual dignity. Sam knew the quail was examining its surroundings before leading the rest of the covey across the road.

"Hell," Sam said, walking on, "y'all just go on and fly. I ain't got time for no politeness. I got too far to go."

The quail, however, merely withdrew into the burdock thicket and Sam went on.

"Could of charmed the last one of them scamps into walkin acrost the road if I had the time," he told himself. "Only maybe they been shot at."

But he was preoccupied and forgot them. He was on his way to see a man named Ruston about a matter of extreme importance and his mind and imagination were crowded with possibilities: how it would be if Ruston said yes, and what were the best ways to get him to say it.

Ruston was a big landowner who worked paid labor. He was, furthermore, a man who'd as soon say no as yes. He was not, like some of the others, known as an especially bad man to work for. He paid trifling wages because it was customary and because a man working in a cotton field is not doing a very valuable thing. He was not known to be vicious or dishonest with his workers beyond the conventional banditry of the commissary system. Neither he nor any of his foremen had killed any Negroes or even quirted any. Grapevine talk said everything he had was mortgaged to the hilt.

And now as Sam walked along the road toward the

commissary, he carefully reviewed the alternatives, carefully thought over what Ruston had to offer. Ruston had one farm of three thousand acres, which meant, of course, that it was a nation, with its own government (Ruston and his overseers), coinage (wages were paid in metal tokens redeemable at the commissary), and civilization. Its citizens lived in a settlement known as a camp. They worked in gangs at the discretion, and under the surveillance, of an overseer on horseback. The workers were separated, the women and girls in one group, the men and boys in another. There was a water cart that followed the gangs, a hoe sharpener, and a mule-drawn privy that ran on skids.

The commissary tokens made you feel bad because you knew they were worth fifteen per cent less than they were supposed to be, since the prices had been jacked up that much. And yet, if you'd really thought the thing through, you knew you were doing as well as when you farmed somewhere on the halves and traded in town on credit. By the time the store got through with you, it had got a little more than fifteen per cent in interest charges; or if you could make arrangements at the bank, the bank got the same fifteen per cent. They got it different ways, made it look cheaper and sound like ten, but they got it. So that canceled out.

There were two things, however, that didn't. One was the overseer. If he were afoot, it would be different. But to have him there all of every day, mounted, looking down at you, shifting in the saddle, was unendurable. No matter how many years you'd known him, you got to hating him, and before long that hating was taking more out of you than the hoe was.

And finally, at the end of the year, whose crop was it? Not legally—you knew the answer to that—but actually. Who had created it? Whose sweat and studying and secret intuition did that crop represent? Why, Ruston's and the gangs'. Which was all right if you happened not to be a farmer, which is to say a man who feels out the darkest of mysteries with the tendrils of his imagination and must watch the result develop and constantly alter his decisions like a commander in the field.

There was no way to cancel out the fact that when autumn came, you had not made a crop, which is a fine thing to have done, but had, instead, only been herded here and there to do the drudgery for another man's plans. Cotton-labor wages were too small to make up to you the emptiness of such a year in which the other man so exclusively got the goody and you got the hull.

Though there was no privacy in the camps, it was pleasant hanging around the blacksmith shop with the others on rainy days or playing dominoes in one of the shacks. Too, there were house dances that formed themselves almost automatically in bad weather. On Sunday there were ball games. And yet there was that hateful son of a bitch on a horse telling you how to hoe corn, or, if not telling you, being there *to* tell you.

But finally, whose crop was it? Not yours.

It was like deciding to have a child and the law said you had to apply to the overseer, which you did, and he happened to be agreeable and said, "O.K., I'll herd the boys right over to your wife and y'all can get busy gettin it started."

It is all right to have a road-working or a cemetery-cleaning and all put in together and get the job done, but some things are private, and none of a lot of co-operative people's business. Unless you happen to be interested only in the financial result.

So Sam was sure he wanted no part of the anonymous civilization of Ruston's three thousand acres.

Fifteen miles from the three thousand, Ruston owned sixty-eight acres in the San Pedro bottoms. Forty acres are supposed to be the maximum one-team family crop of cotton and corn, but somehow Sam had never been as sure of anything as that he was a match for those sixty-eight acres of hillside and bottom. Besides, the character and flavor and spirit of the San Pedro were a thing as definitely and distinctly felt by him as the personality of any of the more interesting of his kin people.

Sam was a river man. And while he could have drawn a precise map of this river's course in detail, in his mind, he did not, preferring to go on thinking of the river as something dark and cool and undulant with mystery, a gauzy shirt to be worn instead of a pill to be taken.

The river would be there, and he had been three years away from the river. And those sixty-eight acres, fertile as the sperm of a goat, were re-seeded by the river each winter with Johnson grass which could be removed only by violence from this goat-rich earth in which its ropy

roots found ever-greater strength and determination to
live stupendously, and to stunt and choke the things a
man might plant there.

Yet he'd hit that Johnson grass so hard and fast with
plow and harrow that even it must perish, for all its
mighty clutching and in-digging.

Ruston would have fine mules, and Sam's mind was
bumped by the great brown-black hemispheres of their
hawser-muscled rumps before him and the plow handles
in his hand, plunging the middle-buster with purposeful
emotion into the black earth, which turned into a Negro
virgin with black thighs twining, and he had to call back
his mind to where he was going, as he would a varmint
dog from a rabbit trail.

Six bits was what Ruston paid, every God's day you
went to the field. And if Nona went too, say, drove a
cultivator or a planter or hoed, that was four bits more.

There would be certainty, for once, at least during the
growing season, that the family would not starve, and
that the river was near, to wind around you when you
wanted and needed it, to baptize you when nothing would
do but you enter it physically.

And the land would be there, stinking and gummy
with a richness which you would tear away from the
weeds and stuff into the corn, the land which you would
enter, plow-wise, with the strength of great mules.

It would be there to be made beautiful with fruit, and
never mind the money part. Ruston would foot the bills.
Your wages would be fixed, and worrying would not
raise them. But to have made the substantial beauty of

cotton and corn, to have studied the signs, and done things when your experience and your sympathy for crops said do it, that would mean you had made the year big with fulfillment and your insides softly luminous with knowing you were right and that as a creature you made sense, and living did.

But first something had to be taken away from Ruston: his belief that you were of sand caliber, because you had worked there. No one would know better than Ruston that the sand attracts people who have not much to give. Because the sand farms easily, with jack-rabbit mules and a Georgia stock. Yet in the end it crushes your spirit more utterly with its bland refusal to give what it does not possess. For it is the loose, incipient mother of nubbins and stunted cotton, and that is all.

And if you live there long, people know how you are, how you must be after it gets through doing what it does to you, and how you probably were when you went there. So your private despair and surrender are no longer a secret if you stay too long in the sand, where even the weeds have no vitality and are easy to kill. This stigma of having worked lately in the sand was what Sam was going to have to keep small in Ruston's mind.

It was also certain how things would be if Ruston said no. Destitution, not comparative, but utter destitution. No money and no credit. Just none at all. And the problem of trying to keep the family alive till spring, which you would manage somehow to do, and not feel too sorry for yourself in the bargain. After all, you'd done it plenty of times before. Then when spring came, you'd begin working a piece of land somewhere on the halves, share-cropping, which you have been doing for the last three years and your returns on days worked have averaged about forty-six cents. If you had got the breaks on weather and price and bugs, you might have done better, but you didn't, and have enough of farming on the halves. The sterility of the land made it like trying to do a good job of half-soling your shoes with paper, and the river was not there.

Sam came up to the commissary steps and saw Ruston talking to a man who must have lived outside the farming world because his pants were not only wool but had a crease in them.

Sam went inside, where some others like himself were waiting in almost hidden nervousness, and asked them a question he knew was important to them all.

"What kind of humor is he in today?"

"I ain't been able to tell," one of them answered, unconsciously going through the motions of warming his hands and buttocks at the cold stove.

There was blue- and plum-colored gingham on the shelves of the store, and kerosene in a square, red crank tank, and snuff and starch and Irish potatoes. There was also a little, glassed-in bin of mixed candy which you wouldn't get much of for a nickel, and flour and lard and sirup.

When Sam's time came, he went over to Ruston, who was short and whose legs bent fatly backward at the knees, and said, "Mr. Ruston, my name's Sam Tucker. I want to go to work for you."

"I'll have to study about that," Ruston said, looking Sam over.

"You send folks from the big place when you need work done on the little San Pedro place, don't you?"

"Yes."

"Well, I been figgerin out how you could save a lot of truck wear and tear, and worrisomeness for yourself, if you'd just let me move onto the little place and work it."

"House ain't any good and you'd have to borrow water because the well's fell in."

"I've done looked it over and know that. But I still want to, anyhow. Been half-and-halfin for the last three years and you know what kind of years they've been. Most of the time we've been whettin pretty much on the point. Just for a year, anyhow, I'd like to day-labor that little place, and know eatin was took care of for a few months. I'd like to raise a crop on that good land that *was* a crop and have some good big mules to do it with."

"Who'd keep your time?"

"I would, and when you drove by every week or so, you'd know whether a week's work had been done just by lookin."

Ruston was still sizing Sam up, knowing that all farmers are hard workers next summer; that, no matter how lazy or unreliable they are, they are moved to great anxiety in the wintertime to make the dirt fly next summer.

"Where've you been farming?"

"Different places."

"Like exactly what place?"

"Well, four years ago I brought in the first bale to

Hackberry and collected the premium. You never saw a sorry farmer bring in the first bale, did you?"

"No, I reckon not."

Ruston thought some more. If this fellow could take over the little farm, which, with its special problems and inconvenient location, was a nuisance, it would be a good thing and would leave him free to concentrate on the big farm.

"You'd be willing to take your money out in trade at the commissary, wouldn't you?" Ruston asked.

"If it was in reach, I would. Don't see how I could hardly walk fifteen miles for groceries and then tote em home."

"I reckon not, either. Look. Here's what I'll do. You don't want to have to walk back over here for an answer, so I'll give you one today. I don't know much about you, but that's a good idea you got for the little place to be run separately. So move on over there and try to stuff up the holes in the house, and I'll take you on a day-to-day basis. By that I mean the first time I come over and don't like the looks of things, I'll fire you and not feel the least bit bad about it. I'll have hands aplenty on the big place and trucks to haul em with and can shoot em over there whenever needed."

Sam grinned. He couldn't help it. All he had to do to hold the little place was what he'd never dreamed of not doing: just farm hell out of it. So easily had he kept the sand years hidden. So easily had the coveted empire of sixty-eight black acres and its ribbon of river fallen into his hands. How firmly and benevolently he would hold it and guide its surging potentialities, its spectacular usefulness! The sixty-eight acres were a wild stallion to be tamed, where the sand had been a spavined old mare that would eat your courage and drink your own vitality and lay back down. He no longer had the impossible task of resurrecting the dead, but of breaking and driving this wild stallion.

"That's a good trade," Sam said. Then, supposing there had better be some official declaration on the matter of payment, he said, "I guess I know what the wages'll be."

"Six bits a day."

"What about my wife?"

"Is she a strong, healthy woman?"

"Yes."

"Four bits. . . . Any kids?"

"None big enough."

"You'll have to hustle, farming that place with just your wife."

"I know. . . . I been figgerin: if you let me have about three dollars a month credit against my first money, me and my folks could kinda scratch along till spring."

"No, sir. Our arrangement is day-to-day. The money starts when the plowing starts. I don't want you all to pick up and leave with your bellies full of my unpaid-for groceries."

Sam laughed. He liked a man who talked like that and didn't beat around the bush.

"Well," he said, "it looks like I'm goin to have to make some other rangements bout feedin my bunch till farmin time."

"Go over there," Ruston said, pointing toward the wooden counter, "and get a dollar's worth of what you need. It's a gift. Always give a new family a dollar's worth. Just a habit of mine. It don't make sense, but I do it. Well, our trade's made."

He told the clerk about the dollar's worth and got in his car and left.

And Sam sure liked that man.

Liking and figuring, he went over to the counter.

A box of .22 hulls for the old gun so he and Zoonie could varmint-hunt for pelts for cash and meat to eat.

Seventeen cents.

Wasn't this marvelous? he kept telling himself. Really unbelievable.

The commissary cornmeal was four cents a pound in bulk and Sam knew where he could get fresh-ground yellow for two cents, but this was white and a gift. He got twelve pounds.

Forty-eight cents.

Plus seventeen.

Made sixty-five. All that meal he had, and fifty hunting bullets.

He got two pounds of lard at fifteen cents a pound. Your belly gets lonesome for grease when there isn't any, and you know there's strength in it and satisfaction when it enriches cornpone.

Now there was a nickel left, and a war began between that mixed candy and a nickel's worth of coffee (the man said he would cover the bottom of a little sack with it for a nickel). But the candy won when he thought of the suffocating excitement in the kids' eyes, of everybody nibbling a piece, including Granny and Nona, and all of them impressed by what a good provider Papa was. Before leaving, however, he got the man to take back one pound of meal in exchange for a fifth of a pound of coffee.

Then he started down the road, and stole a piece of candy out of the sack on the way, but only one very small one.

2

SAM did not go home that night. He had to borrow
a wagon and team to move his family and belongings.
Besides, he was anxious to stop at the Hewitts' and tell the
old man they would soon be neighboring together. Old
man Hewitt was a generation older than Sam. He was tall
and white-headed, wise and circumspect in his ways.
Neighboring with old man Hewitt in this new place was
a consolation to Sam because he knew that, whatever
extraordinary thing happened, the old man would likely
have seen such a happening before and would remember
how it had been dealt with.

Sam was also glad in a way that old man Hewitt's boy
Finley, for whom Sam had no use at all, was going to be

there. Sam didn't like Finley because the only contribution he ever made to the family's comfort was to play an occasional game of dominoes on the shady side of the porch with his mother while the old man worked in the field. Sam could never understand why the old man didn't pick up a chunk and knock hell out of Finley, unless it was out of consideration for Finley's perennial dose of claps, which amounted to a sort of career with him. But if you ever wanted somebody to hold the easy end of a seine or do some trifling thing when everybody else was working, there would always be yellow-skinned, flappy-lipped Fin.

It was almost night when Sam reached the Hewitts'. The old man had a fine little farm and the house was a fairly comfortable one. A wide gallery ran around it like a moat. As Mr. Hewitt held the door open and said, "Come in, come in," Sam smelled cured meat cooking and saw that the Hewitts were glad he'd come. He could tell by the look in Mrs. Hewitt's eyes that the cooking was still in such a stage that more of everything could be added.

So Sam was going to be their neighbor. Well, that was fine.

"I studied about it a long time," Sam said, "and decided I was about due for sort of a vacation. I mean, this way all I'll have to do is the work and the figgerin, but won't have our eats dependin on any one hailstorm or drought or anything like that. Don't aim to do it but this one year, but it looks like a man ought to have that much of a lay-off ever six or eight years."

Old man Hewitt understood perfectly. Once when he was about thirty-five he had done the same thing, and in a way it had worked out and in a way it hadn't. But he knew how rich an experience it would be for Sam to work bottomland. Until he had, no man knew his strength or his weakness.

"What I really stopped by for," Sam said, "outside of seein you all, was to ask if you could spare me your wagon and team to move in."

"For when?" the old man asked.

"For whenever you can spare it."

"I got a load of wood down by the river," the old man said, "which I ain't anxious to have washed away. Spend the night here and we'll haul it up fore breakfast in the mornin and you can take the wagon on."

Two meals that would be. A lot of fried eggs for breakfast, and the Hewitts would have coffee.

"That's mighty nice," Sam said. "Want to, y'all can just go on sleepin in the mornin and I'll get the wood."

"We'll both haul," the old man said, "and drop off half a load over at your house. Most certain there ain't any there, and the first cool breeze comes zizzin through them crackedy walls, you'll need a lot. You can pay me back."

"I'm sure much obliged," Sam said. "Ain't much house, is it?"

"No," the old man said. "Most of our houses is junk, but you couldn't really call that thing a house, hardly. However, I always figgered you was about nine parts Indian and the rest armadillo and could make out sleepin in a ditch if you had to."

"Done it many a cold night sure," Sam said, liking the old man warmly. "Poor Nona's lived around places where just an ordinary hog wouldn't stay. And had kids there, for that matter."

"How is Nona?"

"Middlin, thanks."

"And Granny?"

"Just about the outdoinest thing you ever saw."

"All old folks get that way."

Sam let him go on thinking so.

"This is Sister's second year of school," he said, "and we're mighty proud of how she's doin. Knows her numbers good as the next feller."

"We'll have to catch us some fish this spring," clappy Fin said.

"Course we will," Sam said.

"You're goin to have a struggle with the Johnson grass," the old man said. "The land's poisoned with it."

Sam smiled with comfortable confidence in the warm room, so pleasant with good will and the rich flavor of cured meat frying.

"It ain't frettin me," Sam said, "cause I'm just goin to plow it out. Plow and harrow and plow some more. And draw down my six bits a day. And have the kind of tools that gets the job done. . . ." He sighed. "We're sure goin to enjoy neighborin with you all this year . . . and not be all the time borrowin stuff, either."

"What did you think about Ruston?"

"He's all right," Sam said. "You can tell he's a man that farms bottomland."

Mrs. Hewitt came to the door and said supper was ready, and you knew by the subdued confidence and exhilaration in her face that there would be something left over after everybody had had enough, and that the coffee would be strong.

"We better wash," the old man said.

The washpan sat on a shelf on the side porch beside a gourd dipper and a cedar bucket full of water. They offered Sam the use of the pan first. He was glad he would not have to wash after Finley. Even so, there might be a few bugs left from some other time, but Sam remembered the old saying that only preachers ever caught it that way, and splashed the cold water stunningly on his sharp, leathery face.

The supper was wonderfully big and hot and the biscuits were not made out of relief flour, because they were white instead of blue, and there was an egg custard for dessert. Then, while Mrs. Hewitt washed the dishes, the men talked some more and Sam enjoyed the presence of old man Hewitt's big, gristly nose. You knew a man with a nose like that could only be all right.

Sam asked about the other neighbors, and the old man could think of something good to say for all of them except Henry Devers, which told Sam something. In discussing folk, the old man would generally lay the emphasis on the good things about people because he was, in the first place, the kind of man in whose presence it is hard not to behave yourself and, in the second place, because he was old without being intolerant. But when he didn't say anything at all about Henry Devers, Sam felt certain there was something wrong with him.

"What you countin on doin tween now and farmin time, Sam?" the old man asked.

"Why, I been studyin in the back of my mind kinda," Sam said comfortably, not too full because he had tried to hold onto his manners at supper and not eat these good folks out of house and home. "They've got that there relief in Hackberry. But I ain't much stuck on that. Used to—it was a pretty good bunch durin the real hard times, and a heap o fun, like workin in any gang is—but now it's mostly just culls that don't study nothin but rattin on the job, because the boss can't fire em. Most all of em is friends of mine, either huntin friends or fishin or Saturday-nightin, but it kinda gets my goat to call myself workin and just piss-ant around. Cause if you really put out, it makes the other boys sore and they commence askin you if you want to work, what the hell are you doin there? I mean it's been skimmed down to that, and since this year is to be a kinda play-pretty year, I figgered I'd hit the woods for a livin. Fore long now the fur season'll open, and I ought to could make it till first plowin time by furrin."

"Trappin or doggin?" the old man asked.

"Doggin. I can catch stuff by the leg in traps all right when I have to. But I reckon my nature runs more to huntin."

Mrs. Hewitt had come in.

"There's a heap of pneumonia about," she said, "and

that wintertime huntin is a mighty good way to bring
it on."

"Yes, mam," Sam said. "When I'm doin all this big
catchin I'm talkin about, I'll try to leave that out."

"What have you got for dogs?" the old man asked.

Sam laughed.

"Nothin, hardly. Little ole Spitz, some calls em. Though
I figger thisn's got a shot of rat terrier or somethin in
im. White and fuzzy and weighs about twelve or fifteen
pounds. But that little bugger'll tangle with air coon that
ever walked a log."

"Ole man Christian's got a hound bitch he wants to
give away," clappy Finley said. "She trees short-varmints,
but has commenced killin hogs."

"Much obliged, but unh-unh," Sam said definitely. "I
don't want nothin that bawls on a trail and scares ever-
thin out of the woods. Course they're fine for music-
huntin, but I'm gonna be after fur and meat. I want somethin that don't say nothin till the time comes, and then
says he's up this here very tree I'm barkin up, and
means it."

"What you need is a good cur dog," the old man said.

"They're fine all right, cept folks ain't goin around
givin em away if they been trained any, and I can't hardly
afford to fool with one right now that ain't onto hisself."

Then Finley said let's play dominoes, which Sam did,
badly, because all this talk had stirred his hunting self
from the place where it slept. But presently the game
ended and everybody went to bed. Sam, however, was
careful not to get between the sheets and soil them.

The night passed, quick as the movement of a fish, and it was frosty dawn. Sam and the old man hitched, still waking, and were soon in the gaunt, leafless bottoms loading the wood the old man had cut. And it was just like his nose. There was a lot of it and it was practically all dinner wood, which is to say, sound, hard, long-burning wood, and only a little breakfast wood, willow or box elder or the like, which burns fast and is easy to cut.

When they got back to the Hewitts' house, they unloaded the half the Hewitts were going to keep and went inside, where a breakfast was ready from which a man should have been able to go forth and accomplish anything.

Finley was just beginning to stir about now, with no shirt covering the long drawers in which he'd slept. Dazedly, seeming almost drugged, he rubbed his eyes, trying to slough off the residue of a night's diseased sleep.

The coffee was strong and hot and fragrant, and no part of it was either parched sweet potatoes or parched corn. It went down your throat leisurely, painting your insides with a thick coating of warm delight.

Then it was time for Sam to leave and he did, saying the words of thanks awkwardly. But everybody knew how things were, anyway, and he started off, first to unload his wood, and then to haul his family into that globule of different time, which was to be his play-pretty year.

3

WHEN Sam got home, it was eleven o'clock and the kids climbed all over the wagon and tested everything, including the mules' dispositions. Then in no time, almost, everybody was eating a piece of candy, in sweet sucking wonder, as Sam told them they were moving immediately, and they all marveled at the fact that they were to become black-land people in the twinkling of an eye. They would be by-the-daying it, but they would be doing it in the black land.

"I always knowed we would be somebody one of these days," Granny said. "Pass the candy sack."

Nona didn't say anything, but was pervaded by relief. Not that she worried a great deal, because she did not.

There was always Sam standing between the family and real trouble, but it was a relief to know there would be some certainty in their lives. Nona's face was what some people would call blank.

The kids only knew something big was happening and that they were going to get to ride in that wagon, and ran, throwing their heads back, and got the hysterical sillies.

Nona made a pan of cornbread and there was some left-over boiled rabbit meat, but nobody would sit down to the table to eat. They all ate standing around excitedly, except Granny, who had managed to get her old rawhide-bottomed chair into the wagon and was up there rocking in it, giving orders to people who weren't listening, and giggling because there was no chance of her getting left.

Sam took her a piece of bread.

"You are sure a good boy, Sammy," Granny said. "Always knowed you'd amount to somethin."

"You won't think much of the house, Granny."

"Jess wait till I get my hands on it. I'll have it to where my Frankie wouldn't be shamed to bring company there and set down and eat his dinner."

Her Frankie was the President of the United States.

"You and him," she added affectionately, "y'all are just my boys and that's all they is to it."

"When can we go a good swimmin?" Daisy wanted to know, having heard they were going to the river.

"When it gets warm," Sam said. "You and Brother are sure goin to have fun."

Nona came out with a load of tattered and not entirely clean quilts and told Daisy to get the almanac. Sam got the table and the stools and his ax and the iron bedstead and the hundred-times-mended camp cot Granny slept on.

"Go ahead and tear the guts out of everthing else," Granny said petulantly, tired of waiting. "But please don't destroy my cot. I'll be dead fore long and you can smash it up then. Dead and out of the way," she added bitterly. "Oh, I know old folks is in the way, all right. Know a heap o things I ain't a-tellin, and always said keep the family secrets till the last."

Sam brought the skillet and put it in the wagon.

"You don't love me no more than if I was a yeller dog," Granny said accusingly.

"That's right," Sam said, who seldom listened to her and always agreed with whatever she said.

"Oh, my God," she moaned. "Father in heaven, why did You bring this on me: to be cast out of the heart of my stony grandson?"

"What's the matter, Cutie?" Sam asked.

That tickled her.

"Nothin," she said. "Y'all come on. I'm tard of bein little ole sandy-land trash."

An hour after Sam had arrived with the news, they had cooked and eaten, and loaded their belongings into the borrowed wagon. And another plot of another man's ground which had drunk Sam's sweat was left behind them.

4

As he drove, Sam said to Nona, who was sitting beside him, "I hope you ain't goin to be too much disappointed in the house."

"You said it wasn't nothin extra."

"Reckon it is, though. It's pretty extra bad."

"It's still got two rooms, ain't it?"

"Yeah, but the west one's got a piece of wall missin. Be fine for in the summertime. Cool on that hill, and no real air-tight west wall to hold out the breeze."

"I'd kinda hoped we could have a room to ourselves," Nona said. "I think lots o times Granny ain't sleepin when she lets on to be."

"We can have, when summer comes. Put her and the

kids in that old room with the gappy wall. Or us. And have everthing real nice."

"Any shade trees?"

"Not right at the house. But down at the river there's plenty."

"How far down?"

"Round a quarter of a mile. There's some people got a house bout a hundred yards from ourn. The front of their land runs right up to the back of ours, and it's close like that and their well is the one we'll use."

"Met up with em yet?"

"No. But their name is the Henry Devers."

"Seems like I heard of em."

"And then if you cut across the field, it ain't more'n two hundred and fifty or maybe three hundred yards to the Hewitts'. They loaned us a half a cord of wood."

"I wisht I had me a mess of pickled beets," Granny announced. "I don't want nothin on this green world but some pickled beets. However, some baked backbone would be mighty good with it. . . . Whip em up, Sammy, I'm gettin tard."

"Were they all well?" Nona asked.

"All, I reckon, sides Finley, and he wouldn't tell if he was, for fear somebody might spect him to do somethin."

"Less cook soon as we get there," Granny said. "All this joogin and jostlin has done wore out that little ole piece of bread I et."

In the bed of the wagon Daisy made Jot cry and Nona told her to stop.

"I'm glad he credited you for them groceries," Nona

said to Sam. "Hadn't, I don't hardly know what we'd of done."

"I meant to tell you that fore now," Sam said. "He said our credit wasn't no count with him, and just hauled off and give me a dollar's worth out of the store."

Nona's mouth came ajar.

"It don't make sense," she said, "does it?"

"I reckon. In a way."

In the back of the wagon Daisy, having been scolded, was leaving Jot strictly, disdainfully alone.

Suddenly, with no provocation whatever, he let out a squall, and Nona came to the back of the wagon, up-ended Daisy and spanked her. Then, as the wagon clanked on, Daisy sat there stupefied by this injustice, too proud to try to explain what her mother would not be likely to believe. She just sat there bewildered, her bottom smarting, and cried fitfully. Now she saw Jot was ashamed and sorry for the nasty trick he'd played her, and she knew it was wrong to go on hating him. She was herself ashamed when she refused to relinquish her hate, and cried some more with her face in a quilt until she fell asleep.

Before the spanking, Granny had been angry with Daisy, but the moment Nona started after her to hem her in the corner of the wagon, Granny had got furious and said, "Let my baby girl alone."

Actually the old woman thought of the children as hers, and Sam as hers, and Nona as a servant who, when she interfered in the management of the family, was an impudent intruder.

"Some folks is just mean," she ended her harangue,

"and have got to take out their meanness on poor helpless children. Course everbody in this family is too smart to take my advice about anything, so there ain't no whole lot of stuff gits done right. We don't get nowhere an wear tow-sack drawers."

"You glad of our change?" Sam asked Nona.

"I reckon."

"Poor thing," Sam thought. "She ain't got much pep any more."

But the general spirit in the wagon was still high, for its occupants were going somewhere, and the mules kept a strong pace and broke wind bravely at intervals, as good mules will. An old jingle ran through Sam's mind which said that a mule with this tendency would never tire, a man so constituted was the man to hire.

As they came in sight of the new place, Sam pointed it out and said, "Look at that land."

They all looked.

"She's black, all right!" Granny cried. "Come a good rain, you'd bog plum up to your partickelers. But hit don't differ. We're black-land folks now and you can put that in your pipe and smoke it."

Nona's eyes just saw land that would be hard to farm, and she thought of the incalculable effort a sixty-eight acre, black-land crop would demand from this brood, most of all from the slender, half-fed man beside her. Here was no sand to curl in damp ribbons off a light plow, but gumbo to cling and come up only in great boulders of adhesive earth. A treeless summer and the long hot days in which one grappled with, fought, and clawed at the obstinate, unyielding land from sun till sun. From can to can't. And how you felt when you woke stiff and aching, and your back remembered the hoe and you wanted to crawl away and die. But instead you must go to borrow water with which to cook breakfast.

Sam had come here to pour himself into this recalcitrant, indomitable earth, to make a great crop he could not sell as his own. She could see why he had come, but not how he might bring enthusiasm with him.

As the wagon reached the northeast corner of the farm, where only the road separated it from the river, Sam turned the mules onto the little side road to the left and started westward up the hill, being glad the while that the hole in the house was on the far side and not visible from the big road. However, the house sat unevenly on its askew foundations of wooden blocks and would have looked bad even in the sandy land. Here it was definitely the worst house in the vicinity, not excluding the poor but neat houses of several Negroes who by some extraordinary circumstance owned their own small farms in a settlement a mile or two up the river.

Actually the house was not habitable. The wind had carried off the shingles in patches. In the absence of panes, boards had been nailed over the windows. Its walls had originally been made by nailing one-by-twelves of the proper length vertically onto a frame, the cracks between these boards then being covered by narrow strips, most of which had subsequently fallen off.

"We'll have a dab of house patchin to do, all right," Sam said encouragingly, knowing as he said it, knowing

Nona knew, that it would never be done, that nomads never raise orchards. There would never be time to mend this ancient coop. Besides, why do it for the next fellow? When you are a tenant, you know you'll be gone next year anyway, and somebody else will inherit your lack of care for the land and the houses on the land. If she wants to wash away, let her wash. The landlord will never make any repairs, because the next fellow might want it different; so that in the end these things amount to a conspiracy against the land which feeds the people.

And then they were there, turning into the bare yard, the wagon coming to a grotesque stop, and all of them saw where somebody had defiled this miserable house by letting dung on the front porch. It was a sight, on top of everything else, that curled into you, clawing like the smell of old tires burning, and Granny said, "I ain't gettin out. Whoever done it on the gallery had the right idea. Hit ain't a house, nor even a good crib."

There was a devastating strength about these words because they were true.

Sam knew they were true, but he also knew that this truth was an enemy to the survival of his family, that it wasn't the truth now that was wanted, but courage. It was his final duty to his family at times like this to give them courage by having it. When he had it, they knew it, and it made things seem natural instead of the ordeal they actually were. Something must come out of him now to them and be bigger and firmer and more real than the truth.

He tied the lines to the brake handle and climbed out.

"All right, you snotty-noses," he said to the children. "Hit the ground and rustle some sticks. First thing we're gonna do at our new place is have coffee for everbody. Nona, hand me out the stuff."

"Well, bless Pat if they ain't a graveyard just acrost the road," Granny said, now making out the fallen tombstones among the ragweed. "The Lord just wanted to have it handy, I reckon. Knowed I was too old and delicate to winter in no such sow's nest as this."

Sam and Nona continued unloading the wagon.

"We got anything at all in the way of sweetenin for that coffee?" Sam asked.

A glint came to Nona's eyes like sunlight catching in the nicks of two cheap blue marbles.

"Yes," she said in almost apathetic triumph. "I've had a half a pint of sugar hid off in a jar."

"Father in heaven," Granny moaned, "bring down punishment on em. Not only haul me here to die of sposure like a old mule that's wore his life out for ungrateful folks, but even been hidin goodies."

She was getting on Sam's nerves despite the natural defenses of his system, through which he had become able to hear a smaller proportion of her babble each year, had become able ordinarily to let her nagging pass by him like wind around a tree. But now she was wrecking the spirit of the group when it needed badly to be elevated. He planned not to cross her, but to let her remain where she was in the back of the wagon, to return it to the Hewitts' barn with her sitting there, and even then to leave her in it as long afterward as she cared to stay.

"It ain't much of a man," she remarked, straining her voice so it would carry to the house where Sam and Nona were setting up her cot, "that brings his babies and womenfolks to soak and freeze in no such sin hole as this."

The children came in with armfuls of sticks, and while Sam started the fire Nona went out of the house and found a mesquite bush and broke off a switch that was long and tough. Then she removed the thorns and climbed into the wagon.

When Granny saw her coming over the end gate with the switch, she was a little taken aback, but her habitual certainty that what she did and said were right, that the mere passage of the words through her mouth would change falsehood into truth, that in the end all opposition must collapse before the high, militant righteousness of her glare, now gave her strength.

"Don't you come a-shakin no *mus*-keet switch at me, Nona Macey." (In her moments of more intense disapproval Granny refused to dignify Nona with the name of Tucker, calling her instead by her maiden name, which to Granny was a term of particularly satisfying opprobrium.) "I said it was a sin hole an it *is* a sin hole. I reckon it's good as what you was ever used to. But Sam Tucker ain't a-takin me an my sweet chilren to live in no such slew-footed privy as this. An if there was any manhood in im . . . Don't come no closer to me with that tree limb."

Nona hadn't said anything.

Granny's eyes were growing wide. Fatally, she was

backing farther into the forward end of the wagon, which was surrounded by high side-boards.

Just short of the end of the wagon, however, she made her last stand, straightened herself up like a mad old eagle, looked coldly down at Nona, and, drawing heavily on the megalomania which was a half-realized weapon, she said, "Trash! Don't you dare."

"You can't talk to him like that," Nona said. "Now or no other time. He's got all he can bear. No use tellin you, cause you don't hear other folks' talk. But you're gonna understand me. Ever time you talk mean to him, it's gonna be the same."

And Nona began switching the old woman's legs, driving her into the end of the wagon, where, in order to keep out of harm's way the most recently struck portions of her body, she turned round and round like a roast on a spit, the while raising each foot in turn high and fast, as a reflex initiated by her switch-stung thighs.

"Help!" she was screaming. "Come save me, Sammy boy! She's a-clubbin me to death! Run, Sam! Bring the gun!"

When she ran past Nona to the back of the wagon, Nona laid the switch smartly, repeatedly, on her buttocks. By the time Granny was in a position to jump from the wagon, Sam was there and caught her. Then, so as not to appear to be taking sides before adjudicating this matter, he helped Nona down too.

Granny had galloped across the yard holding her buttocks, and was now on the porch with her dress up, searching for evidences of damage.

"The coffee'll be ready fore long," Sam said, having put it on while Nona went after the switch, and they went inside to get out their cups and spoons.

This was the first time in his thirty-eight years that Sam had ever seen Granny sufficiently surprised or intimidated to be not only speechless but soundless, for in any family dispute she had always been able at least to weep and moan and appear mistreated.

To Sam the world was a more wonderful place. Nona, poor tired drudging gnome, had had that much imagination, was that much of a human, that she could take a switch to that towering old ego which for seventy-odd years had waged tireless, voluble warfare on anyone who had presumed to be her equal, nagging intentionally and unintentionally, steadily undermining the sanity and nervous systems, the power of resistance, of those about her, poisoning them with her restlessness and vague, ceaseless desire to dominate.

As the good coffee went down his throat, Sam couldn't help thinking: "Her butt's stingin this very minute and she ain't sayin a word."

It was sublime. He tried to keep from smiling, but it was useless.

"This is really going to be a year to remember," he thought. "Just broke herself off a switch and went to work."

"Me an Jot want to go with you to take the wagon back," Daisy said.

"All right," he said, and picked them both up by their pants seats and carried them off squealing.

5

SINCE there was still an hour of daylight left after Sam had returned the wagon, he picked up the gun and the cartridges and walked down to the creek. It was winter and a creek hibernates like a bear, but he wanted to go there just the same. The creek does not cease moving in the winter, it just ceases being anything but running water, because the fish are drugged with winter and so are the turtles and the snakes. But it would be there and you could look at it in the future tense and feel how it would be.

He entered the woods at the swimming pool, which was wide and still, its bottom sloping gently from the sand bar on the right. There was a little twelve-foot cliff for the kids to dive off in the summer, hoping everybody was watching and that no sunken logs had moved under the place into which they were going to needle head first.

The water flowed out of this pool across a swift gravel shoal that would be an excellent place later on to seine bait-minnows if you could interest somebody in fishing who had a seine. Areas of tow-sacking pieced together wouldn't do the work. There was not enough screen effect. But maybe you could build a minnow trap if you could find some old screen wire. Yet if you were going to trap, why not trap for the fish themselves? Well, because you were a fisherman, and you would be accepting the respect of fishermen under false pretenses. Because fishing was a thing you did on the river at night and was a rite and a mystery, a thing to which you bent your intuition. And if you were right, you caught them and they were big, and the other men who fished respected you because they knew you had done the thing differently from the great mass who piddle and twiddle and go home with only fisherman's luck, which is understood the world over to mean no fish, a wet ass, and a hungry gut.

And there is a communion among men because it is night on the river and the men are fishermen. The real ones are not just other men, but those who are concerned with a mystery. They are not especially righteous or capable. But they are the kind of people Jesus Christ would naturally traffic with. If He came back, He would hang around with the boys at night and help them catch fish again. You always have to make a little magic to do it right, and you can feel in your bones what's needed, which of course is what He'd do.

But if you are stinking poor, and it's winter, when the fish stir vaguely at the end of a warm spell, and you are in the woods all of every night hunting furs, and you need the fish to feed your gang, you will have no choice but to build a trap. You will have to bait it with whatever you can get, a crow or a rabbit, and tell Nona where it is so she can pull it up every few days and get the fish out if there are any there. But you promise yourself that when spring comes, when it would really slay the fish, you'll take the damn thing out of the water and kick it to pieces. Maybe you're nuts, but that's what you are going to do and you are going to get a lot of pleasure out of busting it up when the time comes.

Walking on down the river, Sam saw a little pile of fresh-cut pecan shells scattered on the ground beneath a squirrel nest in a tall willow. Stopping and squatting on his heels, he searched the tree, starting at the base of each limb and examining it carefully to its end. He was about to get up and go on, after taking a last look at the nest, when he saw a pencil of light, which had been showing through the bottom of the nest, suddenly disappear. So there was a squirrel there and it had moved. Holding the gun in his left hand, he threw pieces of wood at the nest until the squirrel ran up the tree, climbing fast, with its belly close to the bark and its tail flat behind it. It tried to keep the tree trunk between itself and the man, but Sam maneuvered until he could see it peeping around the trunk and shot it.

Supper. Stew with meal dumplings.

Sam stopped at the old buffalo hole. A buffalo hole is any particularly deep and still pool where people dribble corn kernels to attract the big sucking fish three days later when the grain is soft with fragrant rot. Lying on the bank were shreds of corn shucks, bits of cob. Beside this pool, its banks pock-marked by the heels of last summer's poles where they had been driven into the earth, Sam sat down to dress the squirrel and make his plans for the immediate future.

At the first report of the little gun, Zoonie had escaped the children and arrived beside Sam in time to get the warm squirrel entrails. These devoured, he started hunting at once while Sam sat there fitting the necessary pieces of work together into quilts the size of a day.

Tomorrow he must cut wood. Enough to pay back the Hewitts and keep his family for a week or two. Borrow the wagon to haul the Hewitts' wood, and make an extra trip and haul his own. Devote the whole day to fuel.

On the next, hew enough cottonwood strips for the fish trap. Just a sort of chicken coop with a funnel-shaped throat which would allow the fish to enter, but would, once they were inside, prevent them from getting out again. Bait it and take Nona with him when he placed it. And tell her to watch behind her on her trips to it, because clappy Finley had snooping eyes all over him.

Tell old man Hewitt he was available to butcher anybody's hogs for payment in meat, or do fence work for corn, or anything whatever for any valuable consideration. And then . . .

Well, tack some bark strips over the worst holes in the good room of the house. And begin hunting. Make night your day and the woods your domain.

Not hunting, actually, but poaching. The season was not yet open. Hunt and hide the pelts, salted and stretched inside out on wooden paddles, to take to town when the season opened and sell to the dealers, or, if you could wait, to ship to the big dealers in some city and get a better price.

Near by, Zoonie was barking furiously into a bramble thicket and Sam picked up a piece of rotten wood and threw it so that it struck the little dog's rump and shattered.

"Never mind them rabbits, Zoonie," he said. "We're goin to work fore long an it ain't going to be no rabbit-huntin, playin school. You might as well get that straight in your head right now."

Zoonie looked startled, imposed upon, then intelligently comprehending, and trotted off.

As Sam walked on home, he saw a blue bank of clouds in the northwest, and realized he'd been feeling a change in the air for half an hour. He walked faster.

At the house he carried in two loads of the heavy wood and was on his way after the third when the south wind, which had been coming in great gusts, suddenly died, and he felt a heavy pressure against his chest. This was the interval in which the wind god was throwing the switch. Sam stood there looking into the low, now black, cloud bank and began counting. At the count of twelve he heard a distant but very grand roar, like a fleet of freight trains charging up a hill. Then he saw frenzy passing up the bottoms, saw the bare limbs of the great trees begin thrashing, and a dark, blue-gray curtain following not far behind. It was a thrilling sight, somehow, to watch the storm come step by powerful step, but there was just time to get into the house with one more load of wood before the rain came.

When he staggered through the door with his hundred-pound burden, the wind, like a big hand, pushed him inside. Then while Sam made a fire in the fireplace, the children had a shivering contest and got the sillies, with Daisy taking the initiative, and carefully trying to work Jot into a state of gibbering hysterics. It was just something to do.

"Well, I ain't sayin nothin," Granny was muttering darkly, "but you see what *He* thinks about it. Says, 'Honor thy father and mother that thy days may be long.' Just as apt as not to blow the ole rattletrap plumb offen the blocks. Cept ole Mr. Buzzard-Puke Devil's got his hand in it too. Got it fixed where that there wind can't get no real good holt cause it just passes right on through."

The squirrel was in a pot with cornmeal dumplings at the edge of the galloping fire and the children were playing a new game in which you went up to this big fire to warm yourself and pretended the blast of its heat sent you swooning backward.

Already, in half an hour, the temperature had dropped fifteen degrees outside and it was cold inside the house if you got more than five or six feet from the fireplace, within which area the rain, providentially, did not pour. Most of the rest of the room was flooded, and Granny's cot stood on top of the bed, which had been moved onto a small, sheltered island near one corner. Both the cot and the bed were loaded with articles that must not be allowed to get wet.

Sam was breaking a dozen matches in two so they would fit into a tin, five-cent snuff box and there keep dry.

"I'm just tard of eatin meat that ain't got no real seasonin to it," Granny whined. "What our stew needs is a good double handful of chopped-up onions."

"Just be patient," Sam said. "Fore too long the whole bottoms will be strewed with wild onions and the nights will be rotten with the stink of em."

"Sammy boy."

It was plain by this suddenly affectionate approach she was going to ask for something.

"What, Granny?"

"Fore too very long the Lord's gonna take me away."

"He ain't. But go ahead."

"I say He is."

"Ain't nobody goin to take you nowheres till you get ready to go, and you know it."

"Shut up your sassy mouth," she said sharply, then said, "I got more over across the Jerden than's left down here."

And that sentence rose above her endless burble and meant something true and tragic, and it twisted Sam's heart. The old woman's eyes misted. For a moment she was a lost creature who had lived past her time and the death of her loved ones. Then without effort the mood was gone as the really insatiable greed of her belly crowded it out of existence.

"I just want to hold on till good spring," she said, "when the wild polk greens commence growin out of the ditches, and get you to pick me a good mess and boil em up with a piece of nice fat meat."

"And have the whole family a-lopin round this bare hill with the polk salad squirts."

"Not if you pare-boil em first and throw away that first water. It's that old first water that throws your bowels in a uproar."

"All right," Sam said. "It's a promise."

By now the stew was ready and Nona dished it up and passed the plates around.

"Hold on a minute," Sam said. "We're a-goin to have a blessin."

"How come?" Granny said. "I taken the Lord to be a stranger in this house."

"I just feel good," Sam said, then bowed his head and said, "Much obliged, God. I believe we're goin to make the grade. Amen."

Everybody, including Sam, was a little shocked at this sudden, spontaneous religious impulse.

In quiet hunger they ate their supper.

6

WHEN dawn came, Sam had been waiting for it. The children had slept with him and Nona because there was neither a dry place to make their pallet nor enough cover. As it was, they had slept warmly, if crowded, and Granny's cot had occupied that dry lip of floor in front of the hearth and the banked fire. As Sam waited for the day, he could hear her steady exhalations through relaxed, flappy lips.

The rain had been prodigious, but now had stopped. The bottoms would be a mire and the river would be well up. The temperature, he guessed, must now be something like twenty-five, but he saw no reason to alter his plans, and was warmed by the thought that yesterday's plan-

ning would, despite the churlishness of the weather, be
today's fact. To a minor extent it had even played into
his hands. He had expected to lose time at the well, where
he would go for a couple of buckets of water, and where
he would have to introduce himself to the Deverses and
chat a while and make arrangements to go on using their
well. Now, however, he not only had two buckets of
water but every pan and crock full of rain water caught
from the leaks, and that only after the roof had been
washed down by the first flooding burst of rain. There
was an old file on the mantelpiece that was almost as tooth-
less as Granny, but with this he would sharpen his ax
while Nona got breakfast.

Already, through a cold crack in the wall he could see
a kind of grayness in the east, but he knew it might be a
white cloud or a mirage fostered by impatience, and so
waited a little longer until he was sure that good daylight
was only half an hour away. Then he got up and stepped
into his pants and shoes, having slept in his shirt and ragged
drawers for warmth. Now he went out on the porch, as
he did every morning of his life, to wet off the edge of
it and survey the day, since its character usually deter-
mined what he would do. As he stood there, the north
wind cut into him and he shivered. Anticipating the day-
long soaking his feet would get, his toes curled shrink-
ingly.

He went back inside the house to scrape the ashes off
the popping embers and to pile on wood. When this mass
was still slow about burning, he took the ax into the other
room and chopped a few slivers of pine from the half-

fallen wall. These were damp but quickly dried, and in a few minutes he had made again the old and important miracle of fire, which was now leaping redly, blue-yellow and hot, in the fireplace, and charming the others out of bed.

Zoonie, the little white dog, got down from the seat of Granny's chair where he had been sleeping. It had been pushed under the table, the top of which had served Zoonie as a secondary roof. Now he came and lay, luxurious with warmth and sleepiness, on the hearth.

By this time Nona was making bread and, conscious of what Sam must face today, was generous with the lard in which she fried it. The two-pound package Ruston had given them was all they had, but today was more real and immediate than the future, and must be dealt with now.

"I just hope to the good Lord you got more sense than to go out in any such weather as this," Granny said to Sam, not deigning to be concerned with whether it was necessary or not.

"Got to cut a little wood to keep you folks warm," Sam said, knowing that if he brought to her attention its direct benefit to her there would be much less said.

"Well, it's a mighty mean day, shore," the old woman said and let it go at that.

"What about Sister goin to school?" Nona asked.

"She can catch the bus down at the big road," Sam said. "If it ain't rainin, she might as well, I reckon. Tell me them teachers make em dry out good when they get there."

"She ain't got any coat with any warmth to it," Nona said, staring expressionlessly at the fact.

Sam stopped eating his bread and thought into the fire. That the kids be educated, by which he meant get through public school, was a sort of automatic vow of his so actual and definite that he'd never had to take it. Real literacy was a mysterious realm in which his betters lived and into which he was going to maneuver his children. The fact that he could do this for them if he tried hard enough had always seemed astonishing and uncannily wonderful to him.

"She's got to be coated and sent," Sam said.

Nobody said anything. He was raving, they felt, and they must let him rave himself, finally, into acceptance of the inevitable. A coat is decidedly something you cannot wish into existence.

"It's a long time till the bus runs," Sam said, and got out his knife and whetted it on his shoe. "Bring me that best blanket off of Granny's bed."

In a flash Granny was standing up, shrieking in horror.

"Sam Tucker, you crazy thing, you're out of your head! Ain't nobody gonna lay one finger on that good blanket."

Sam stood up and got it. And in the getting, there was a thing that subdued the old woman, that hammered her into silence.

"Thread me a needle," Sam told Nona. Then to Daisy he said, "Come ere, Sugar."

She came and he measured her arms. Next he cut a long

strip from the blanket that, when folded over, fitted around them. Then he cut the long strip in two and told Nona to sew the two strips into sleeves.

"They're too long," she said.

"There's goin to be cuffs," Sam said, and wrapped the blanket around Daisy's body, saw how much was needed, and cut it off. Next he cut armholes, and just above them cut out triangular patches pointing to them, and when she stuck her arms through the holes and he held the tips of the absent triangles together, there were shoulders to the thing. When these shoulder seams had been sewed, he cut a band to fit around her neck and folded it double and sewed this on so that it would protect her throat. It stood up straight and trim, like the collar on a soldier's dress coat. Finally he cut a shield-shaped patch for a pocket, and took the five brass buttons off his jumper.

"Sew these on," he told Nona.

Then at the right length they made a hem on this object that had been a blue blanket, and it looked so good Sam kissed Nona.

When Daisy had put on and buttoned her coat and had her bread wrapped up and her books under her arm, all the rest of the family walked around her silently, looking, being gratified by the fact that the new garment really looked like a coat. Somehow all the firmness of Sam's intention had registered itself in the finished product so that it was not doubtful or in any respect accidental. It was exactly what had not existed an hour and a half earlier: an integrated, self-confident coat.

Sam picked up his ax and set Daisy on his shoulder and

started down to the road, knowing he had done a thing
that worked and that there was still half of the blanket,
longways, for Granny to cover up with.

Soon the bus came. He put Daisy on it with the chatter-
ing, shivering kids and waved at all of them. Then the bus
was bouncing on, taking Daisy to be doctored for her
ignorance, to be injected with wisdom, and he turned
and went on to the woods, singing:

> *Two wheels up and two wheels a-draggin,*
> *An you can't ride in my little waggin. . . .*

This freezing, muddy morning it was marvelous to be
alive.

Sam bogged along the river bank, noticing that the
river was up a couple of feet and seeing by the line of
flotsam and flattened weeds on the bank that it had been
three feet higher during the night. He was on his way to
a certain elm he'd seen yesterday that had been ringed
earlier and now was dead. But as he came up to it, he
heard sounds of chopping and saw a red-headed youngster
hacking away at its butt.

"Hello there," Sam said.

"Mornin," the boy said.

"How come you to be over here cuttin wood?"

"Papa said to."

"Who's Papa?"

"Henry Devers."

"I'm Sam Tucker, you all's new neighbor. What's your
name, son?"

"Bucky."

"Well, don't that next-door piece of bottom belong to y'all?"

"Yes, sir."

"Well, how come he never sent you there to cut? Been handier."

"I don't know, sir. He just never."

"Don't you go to school?"

"Some."

"I guess he'll be on down here fore long to chop with you."

"No, sir. Said he had some stuff to do around the house."

"Well," Sam thought, "if that don't take the rag offen the bush, I don't know what does. Sendin that child out in this weather to cut wood and him up there settin on his bird-dog ass by the fire."

Like any boy with red hair, Bucky had a winning way. Sam wished there were something he could do about getting the kid in out of the cold, but he couldn't. After all, Henry Devers was the man they would depend on for water.

"Well, go ahead and give it hell," Sam said. "I'd kinda took aim on that one myself, but I'll find me another. Try not to let it fall on you."

There was a look of gratitude in the boy's eyes that was not simple. He seemed to guess Sam realized he had been sent here to do a thing he knew was wrong and foolish, but one that he dare not refuse to do.

Sam went on until he found another tree, a dead hackberry, and went to work, felling, trimming, chopping off the limbs, then splitting the trunk.

By four that afternoon he passed Bucky still chopping and said, "Well, I'm goin to call myself got enough cut and do a little haulin."

Bucky grinned, tired and cold, just nodded, and went on working.

By nightfall Sam had finished hauling and had returned the team. Then while he ate his bread it began raining again and he was thankful it had waited until he got his wood safely up on the hill.

Daisy came and hooked her elbows over his thighs and played jumping her feet off the floor.

"Your coat done good," she said. "I gathered me up some little stuff to carry in the pocket."

"I'm proud of it, all right," Sam said, getting ready to make his fish trap. Since there weren't any nails, he was burning holes in the slivers of wood in order to lace them together with baling wire.

"That thing'll bring the law down on us," Granny said unforcefully, divided between her desire to prophesy a little doom and her equally strong one for a good mess of fried fish.

"It ain't likely," Sam said. "Besides, everthing's a chance."

The rain now was falling with such great force that it shook the house.

Suddenly Sam said, "I've changed my plans. This here rain done it."

In Nona's eyes there was a look of mild, patient interrogation.

"It's done rained to where a person'd bog out of sight

in these old bottoms. Sides, the creek'll come out tomorrow, maybe tonight, so here's what I aim to do. I'm goin
to net for buffalo in the mornin, and if catchin is good,
start to the sand hills below Hackberry tomorrow afternoon and do my huntin there."

Sam was thrilled by this turn of affairs.

"I don't know of nothin you've lost in them sand hills,"
Granny said.

Well, Sam didn't either, except his boyhood, so he
didn't answer her.

"Get Papa down his net," he said to Daisy. "We got to
have a patchin."

The net was old and home-made, woven of No. 8 black
cotton sewing thread. It was an instrument that could be
used only under special circumstances, but if conditions
were right it could do wonderful things. In half an hour
it had been repaired and Sam was counting on wetness to
increase its now rot-depleted strength to a point where
it would do the job.

"Folks will drive out from town to see how high the
river's rose," Sam said, "and I'm nelly cinched to catch
a ride far as Hackberry."

"Tell all the kinfolks hello," Nona said, "and ask for
the news."

"Was it me goin down there amongst all them kindred," Granny said, getting into bed, "I'd come home
with me a sack of good sweet taters and some goobers and
I don't know what all."

"We'll see," Sam said, and covered the fire with ashes.

And then they all were in bed and the room was dark,

but the children still could not sleep on the floor, so despite the fact he was going on a journey tomorrow away from his wife, Sam closed his eyes and went to sleep.

The night rushed past in the confusion of his tired-man's sleep and it was dawn again, and fire and bread were made. Daisy wanted to go with her father to the river, but must stay and gaze into those dead textbooks, studying her lessons until time to catch the bus. Sam kissed her and left.

From the hill on which the house sat, Sam could see not only the rushing, brown-yellow band of the San Pedro, but to the south could see another creek which effected a confluence with the San Pedro six miles farther down. Thistle Creek was a far worse actor than the San Pedro and was all over everything. He had known it would be, and having confirmed this fact walked on to a slough which ran out from the San Pedro. The river now was running bank-full, swirling and sucking muddily, slamming driftwood into everything. It seemed, nevertheless, to have reached the peak of its rise, for the slough was full and without any current whatever.

Which was an excellent, propitious state of things. When Sam found two saplings growing out of the slough at the proper distance apart, he dragged a log to the edge of the water and floated one end of it across so that it would catch in a notch in the far bank. Then he tied his net to the sapling on the east bank, cooned the log, holding the other end of the net in his mouth, and finally fastened it to the sapling on the west bank.

This done, he sat down on a stump, his body waiting,

his imagination seeing a big buffalo fish, with down-turned hog snout, feeling its way along the river bank for some exit from this maelstrom of swirling mud, searching for a place where the water would be still and already in the process of settling. A very big buffalo this one was, white and ready to gleam when the light reached it; patiently searching, up-current always, like a plane landing into the wind, else its control would be gone and the current would bang it into things; up-streaming toughly like a hog looking for what it wants, a hog whose snout is turned toothlessly down, a tapir fish. On up the river it swims until it finds the slough out of which no current thrusts against it, and the water is settling, and soonest will be clear. And it comes out into the still water gliding, the pressure off, and touches the net, so gauzy a web with its three-inch mesh, hanging slack and unweighted, by no current tightened, that it is unnoteworthy to this tapir fish which is wont to burrow through great drifts after what it wants. And the fish continues, until it begins to sense the gentle increase of pressure, and charges in some direction, frantically, while this strange cobweb, like the thousand restraining strands of the Lilliputians, enfolds it, there to be held until removed by a strange monster who wears his head upon a terrifying extension, and all the thrashing of a strong, cogent, thick-scaled body will not be enough to win release.

Then, abandoning this reverie, Sam saw in actuality a red boat turning forlornly in an eddy at the edge of the stream, and with a pole captured it. Evidently it had been wrenched from its mooring somewhere up the river. In it was what could not be. What simply could not just come drifting down the muddy river to him in a runaway skiff. It was beyond belief and beyond happening. There, floating in that three-quarter-filled boat, dry inside its cellophane covering, was a package of cigarettes.

How long had it been since he'd had so much as a little sack of Durham?

His lungs glowed.

Then he noticed two smooth sticks protruding over the seat that might be the handles of something so necessary to his life that he dared not hope it might be that. And he lifted it up and, by God, that was what it was! A minnow seine. And when it continued to unroll, each turn of the handles alive with suspense, he knew it was a twenty-footer, and saw there were but three perfectly patchable holes in it, and that none of these was in the middle.

Sam stood there looking at this miracle and lit a cigarette. He took an enormous pull, feeling the smoke swirl down into his lungs, and his head grew suddenly, sharply, beyond pleasantness, dizzy and he knew he had been a pig in his eagerness.

He dragged the boat ashore and tied its short, broken chain to an overhanging tree limb in such a way that it could weather an additional five-foot rise.

Sam carried his treasures to the set-out net, which he now saw hanging tighter than when he had left it, and removed a twelve-pound buffalo. A twelve-pound buffalo was a good fish, but not exceptional. Under five pounds they were hardly edible, being little more than a mass of bones. But a twelve-pounder, dressed by an expert, would be splendid.

In order to keep the fish alive indefinitely, he did not string it through mouth and gill, but made a halter on its head as you would upon a horse, the gills preventing it from coming off forward, the snout loop too small to slide backward over the body, and staked it there, to attend his pleasure.

If the owner inquired for the boat, he might take it, but God had given Sam the seine and the cigarettes, and he meant to keep them and use them and tell the boat man so. They could be called salvage fees.

Of the four fish that he took before noon, there was a twin to the twelve-pounder, and a baby of six, and another which Sam knew would weigh eighteen pounds, but which his pride called twenty-one.

Sam thought of his neighbor, whom as yet he had not met but must depend on for water, and decided to give him the six-pound fish. One of the twelves would last his own family a couple of days, and the other two he would sell in town.

He started home, leaving the two selling fish staked out and his net in the water. He was eager to get to the sand hills, but buffalo fish are money; the river would not start falling fast until late in the afternoon and he must carry to town as many as he could catch.

Now as he walked up the hill to the house he began to make stirring changes of plan which were full of niceties and shadings.

Leaving a twelve-pounder at home, Nona proud, and Granny in a frenzy of lip-smacking excitement, he took the six-pounder to Henry Devers's house and called hello.

The man who came out was tall. His clothes were dry and his eyes were set close together. He was chewing.

"What is it?" he said.

"I'm your next-door neighbor," Sam said. "I thought you might want this little fish. He ain't much, but would make a real fine soup."

"You mean do I want to buy him?"

"Oh, no," Sam said, laughing, but embarrassed. "He's not hardly a good give-away fish."

After a second of thinking, Henry Devers said, "All right. If you haven't got any use for him, we'll take him."

The son of a bitch wouldn't accept it as a neighborly gift, but was trying to make it seem like he was doing you a favor.

"I guess my wife'll be over here before long wanting to borrow water from your well," Sam said, now having to try hard.

"It's all right, long as there's plenty of water," Devers said. "This summer you may have to make some other arrangements. Gets pretty weak in dry weather. We'll take time about on the rope wearin out."

Sam's eyes looked at the worn-out thing now run through the well pulley, felt himself getting angry, and knew he'd better go.

"Well, so long," he said. "My wife's cooking us a fish and I'm about ready for it."

"I ain't no netter," Henry Devers said self-righteously. "I fish hook and line."

"Sure nuff?" Sam said, then said, "So long" again and left.

His own house smelt marvelously of baking fish. He was glad to be there and away from the presence of his neighbor.

"You done real good on your fishin, Sammy," Granny said. "You're a sweet boy and I love you."

"I left my net out," Sam said. "I'm goin to try to catch some more this afternoon and sell em in town. Now if I do, there'll be some money and I don't want to bring it plumb back out here. So I'll buy groceries with it and leave em at the store, at Brandon and Neely's, and Daisy can haul em home on the bus."

"The store'll grab the money," Nona said, "for what we owe em."

"I'll talk to Russell about it," Sam said. "If he won't agree, I'll buy em somewhere else and bring em home. What do you need?"

"A little flour and a piece of salt jowl meat and a few sirup and a pinch of bakin powder is what we need worst," Nona said. "That's an awful lot to come out of any little fish-money, but you asked me."

"Don't send me no nickel can of snuff for my nerves," Granny said. "Do, I might die from over-happiness."

"I'll do the best I can," Sam said. "If it keeps on cold like this, maybe you all better bunk up together. I'll be home fore it's time to do any plowin, which'll be the first good dry spell of weather."

"This afternoon you're leavin?" Nona asked.

"Yes."

She carried Granny's chair and some blankets out on the porch. Then she hung another blanket over the wide-cracked wall between the porch and room and said, "Take Jot out there and wrap up and sit with him a while."

"It's too cold," Granny said. "Sides, it looks like to me . . ."

Nona went quietly to the mesquite bush outside and broke a switch, but when she got back Granny and Jot were on the front porch.

Nona put a chair against the door and got out of her clothes.

7

AT three o'clock that afternoon Sam heard a car
coming from the direction of Hackberry and began to
take up his net. The car, he knew, would be able to drive
but a little way beside the river before reaching a low
place in the road that would be under water. He'd have
to catch that car as it turned back to town. Besides, he
now had four fish weighing twelve or more pounds each,
and fish, this far inland, were magic. He would not need
to hail the car, just stand beside the road holding the fish,
and the driver would stop to admire them, to ask, probably, what kind they were, where and how they had been
caught.

When the car came over the hill, Sam saw it was a

pick-up truck, which was better still. He put the squeezed-out net in its little cloth draw-string bag, tied it to his belt, and was standing by the road in plenty of time.

The driver of the truck, as it happened, was Dave Lock, a giant of six feet five, who had recently moved from the post oak range in to Hackberry and was a dealer in live-stock.

At the very thought of riding to town with Dave Lock, Sam grinned.

Dave drove up and stopped.

"Get in this car," he said, "and tell me how you caught all those fish."

"Oh, just nettin around," Sam said, putting the fish and Zoonie in the back. "How you like bein a town man?"

"All right. Fine."

"You doin any good buyin stock?"

"Pretty, I reckon," Dave said.

"I know you right well," Sam said, "and guess you don't like to talk about it" (Sam's face was wreathed in involuntary smiles), "but ever time I think of that whippin you gave that whole beer joint full of sons of bitches that night in town I just feel good all over."

"I don't reckon it was so very smart," Dave said. "A man ought to be able to settle his business peacefully."

"Cordin to who you're dealin with," Sam said. "Them bastards knew you could beat the Jesus out of em if you was a mind to. They just thought you'd go on tryin to persuade em by beggin em to do right. Knew you didn't like to hurt nobody. They'd of gone on stealin your stuff an doin you dirt forever if you hadn't done just what you done."

"I'll say this much," Dave said. "When I was doin it, everything inside of me said I was doin right. Maybe that counts for something."

"It was just flat-footed wonderful," Sam said. "And the way you stood up to them hen-house policemen with your belly shot open, knocking hell out of em! I've wished a hundred times you could of gone on and whipped them too. You did, of course. But I mean had em layin out in the floor with their pistols restin on their chests like lilies. That way it'd been really perfect."

"I'm just glad it's all over," Dave said, "and that nobody got killed."

"Reminds me so much of one time when I was younger and workin with a road gang in Oklahoma," Sam said. "Local folks had dances around and it came up a kind of bad feelin tween us and them. Diddlin trouble of some kind, seems like. Anyhow, the leader of us says this night we're goin to take these hayseeds in, and started it at the dance. One of the outdoinest fights that ever took place and I came through it better'n any of em. Only feller didn't get a scratch. Cause when it started, I just eased downstairs of this big ole barn and crawled in the manger and rested there on that soft hay listenin to the ruckus goin on upstairs. . . . Says many are called and few are chosen. But that go-round I never felt called on."

Dave laughed.

"How's Ethel?" Sam asked, referring to Dave's wife.

"All right. We're fixin to have us a youngster."

"Well, good for you all," Sam said. "He ort to be a real dinger, comin out of such folks as you an Ethel. Please tell er I said hello and good luck."

"She'll preciate it."

Dave asked what Sam was doing this year and Sam told him.

"I'd like it if you'd pick you out one of them fish," Sam said.

Dave did not want to accept as a gift what Sam had to sell, yet to offer to pay for the fish would certainly hurt Sam's feelings.

"That's mighty nice," Dave said, "but we're leavin town this afternoon and it'd rot fore we got back. Thanks a lot, just the same."

Now they were coming into Hackberry and Dave said, "Where'd you like to get out?"

"Somewhere not right downtown. You're sposed to have a license to sell fish, which I ain't got, so I'll peddle these down in nigger town."

Dave drove him there. Sam thanked him and left the truck, and by the time it was gone, the black faces, with eyes full of big-fish wonder, were converging on him.

"Where'd you get em, boss?"

"San Pedro."

"When?"

"Today."

"One of them there nets?"

"That's right."

A moment of silence. Then the question that mattered. "How much?"

"Dime a pound."

"With the haid on and guts in?"

"Take the guts out but the head stays on."

"What they weigh?"

Sam told them and he knew what he told them was right. You come to know exactly what fish weigh.

"That ole big un's too big. He'll taste cose. He ought to be bout a nickel a pound."

"A dollar bill'll buy him," Sam said. "That's a heap o meat for a dollar."

It was. Pools of dimes and nickels and quarters were made up until each fish was sold.

In forty-five minutes Sam had three dollars and twenty cents in place of the fish, and he and the Negroes were mutually delighted with their bargains. Already Sam's customers were on their way to cook their fish, mealtime for the Hackberry Negroes being any time when there was something to eat.

Sam crossed the tracks and walked up the newly paved streets among the to him opulent-seeming houses, all of which he felt would be marvelously tight against the north wind, would have warm fires going, and sheets and dry cover on the beds. He was cold and his mind had to squint to hold a cup of steaming coffee in its field of vision and to exclude the sharp, throat-burning, gut-warming, soul-lifting thought of a thirty-five-cent half-pint of whisky. The whole inside of him was set aquiver by this scalding, sweet, red-brown, contraband thought which argued that the fish were all a piece of luck and what was thirty-five cents. But there was always the danger that after half a pint you might do something reckless and foolish. Might spend the rest on the old tarts that hung around the beer joint. Or maybe just sit down and eat the whole thing up in hamburgers. But if you left the other money somewhere else first, so you couldn't get it back . . .

He was growing excited now because he was making the whisky decently feasible.

On he walked, on feet not believing the smoothness of pavement, through the store section of Hackberry, his excitement displacing almost entirely the sense of peasanthood which he always felt in town, and went to Brandon and Neely's, where a burr-headed young man was scurrying about trying to make the place make money.

Sam went up to him.

"Hello, Sam," Russell said. "What's on your mind?"

"I know about those six dollars I been owin you for three years, Russell, and got a little change in my pocket and nothin to eat at home. I got to spend that money on groceries somewhere and get the groceries. What I wanted to do was cash-buy em here and let my girl pick em up tomorrow, cause I'm goin to the sand hills after fur. Would that be all right?"

"Why, hell, yes," Russell said. "What do you think I am, anyway?"

"Well, three years is kind of a long time to owe six dollars."

"Next thing to forever," Russell said. "Get your stuff and set it aside. How's your folks?"

"Pretty good."

"If you see your cousin Luke down in the sand hills,

tell him I've heard that those pigs of his he mortgaged to me for groceries are fixin to get in bad health and die. Tell him I know two places where he's already tried to sell em, and that if he does I'm going to slap his butt into the penitentiary."

"Luke ortent to do a thing like that."

"Just tell him," Russell said. "It'll be a nice thing for him to know beforehand."

Sam said he would, and Russell, with electric nervousness, was gone somewhere else doing something else.

Sam bought flour, six pounds; sow belly, three; sirup, one gallon, by God, for fifty-nine cents, because you get tired of never having anything sweet; a fifteen-cent pound of coffee; eight pounds of Rio Grande Valley winter cabbage, at two cents a pound; a nickel's worth of Granny-snuff; a can of dime tobacco and some gimme papers for himself; a nickel box of matches; four cents' worth of salt. At five cents a pound, onions were too high to think about, but pinto beans were not, and soaking would swell them. He bought fifteen cents' worth—all that, he'd bought for two dollars and five cents—and a nickel's worth of garlic, which was stronger than onions and would go further, made two ten. Plus a dime's worth of baking powder. That and a remnant of good fifteen-cent cloth for anything that suited Nona's fancy, and a nickel spool of thread to match, brought it to two-seventy. Well, add a dime's worth of mixed candy, and four little oranges for a nickel.

By jucks, it was a real gob of groceries. It would keep the Tuckers' bellies full till he got home from hunting.

He would leave them rich in coffee and candy and cabbage and meat. Already he could sense the warmth that all of them would feel for him when they saw the abundance he'd sent them.

Now he walked outside with thirty-five cents to spend for whisky, singing inside with clean triumph and expectation.

Sam drank his whisky and got some restaurant scraps for Zoonie which they shared in the alley, and at a reasonable hour caught a ride going south, having, on his modest spree, neither fought nor fallen down, nor even hollered. He had merely walked the streets for a while in great physical and spiritual contentment, then gone to the domino hall, where, after watching a few good games, he had got a lift with Ed Rankin.

Ed's car was just a bodiless chassis and Sam had to sit with him on the gasoline tank, holding Zoonie and the gun in his arms. Since there was no muffler, conversation was next to impossible, but with sullen Ed it was never easy anyhow.

"Rode into town with Dave Lock today," Sam shouted once. "We got to talkin about that beer-joint whippin he gave you Red Hill boys that time."

No answer.

On, nakedly, they rode through the freezing night.

Later Sam called, "How's your grandpappy?"

"Just the same. Meaner'n a son of a bitch. Tried to rape a little Mexican girl last week and she split his head with a rock."

Sam could see a soft smile come on Ed's face at the thought of Grandpappy getting his head peeled.

At the turn-off to Red Hill, Sam left the car and went on afoot with the cold wind pushing him from behind. Just before midnight, he came up to the yard of his mother's house. He held Zoonie under one arm to keep him from being devoured by Zeke, a big, shaggy half-bloodhound-and-half-collie, and a white-and-yellow cur with whom Sam was not acquainted.

Actually Sam thought Zeke recognized him but refused to be outdone in ferocity by the other dog. Anyway, they held him at bay until Harmie Jenkins, Mamma's present husband, came to the door and said, "What is it?"

"It's me," Sam said. "Call off these here lions and tigers."

Harmie did and Sam set Zoonie down, and he was so small that the other dogs felt in no way endangered and therefore did not try to kill him.

"Well, what's new?" Harmie asked, snug in his long drawers.

"Nothin much. Just thought I'd come a-huntin if I won't be in y'all's way."

"Not a bit," Harmie said as they paused beside the soft broad warmth of the banked fire. "That old yeller dog out there's sposed to tree."

"Well, you go on and get your rest," Sam said. "We'll talk in the mornin."

"Who's that out there you're talkin to, Harmie?" Mamma called.

"Sam."

"What's happened?"

"Nothin. He just came a-huntin."

"Well, that's real nice. My possum tooth's been a-botherin me lately. And Harmie won't hunt. Y'all get to bed."

"I ain't even offered to make coffee," Harmie said.

"That's too much trouble," Sam said, with moderate conviction.

"We got it here to make."

"Let's wait till about breakfast time."

They went to bed, Sam wondering if his family were warm and safe, and supposing that they were. Again he realized the feeling of fortification Nona would have tomorrow when she saw all those groceries come pouring out of the school bus, and particularly that whole gallon bucket of sirup.

He fell asleep.

8

WHEN Sam awoke the next morning, he remembered happily where he was and was soon dressed and following a trail of rich cooking smells to the kitchen.

"You reckon that's enough meat?" Harmie was asking. And Mamma, big, dark-skinned, churn-butted Mamma, was saying, "No. That boy can eat the behind out of a wildcat when he's a mind to, and this good cold mornin'll have him ready."

"Mornin, everbody," Sam said.

That included the scramble of kids, some of them Sam's full brothers and sisters, some only half. But all of them knew him and liked him, and he could tell by the glitter in the boys' eyes that they knew he had come hunting.

Mamma kissed him, said, "Praise the Lord," and went on frying meat.

"We are sure glad you came," Harmie said to his stepson, who was about his own age, as Sam took his seat at the breakfast table.

Harmie was a man with sandy hair and large bodily members. Sam had always liked him, and felt beholden to him for marrying Mamma and thereby putting a stop to her churchyard and cotton-row trysts with most anybody that offered. Because Mamma was a prodigious creature and it wasn't anybody's fault. She just was. She was marvelously strong, and when not under the spell of some powerful emotional impulse had pretty good sense. Under emotional stress she might do anything, and had done a lot. When she went to the mourners' bench to testify, congregations fell hungrily silent, because they knew that, unlike themselves, she was going to tell the truth and that the truth about her would be virile and compelling.

She had particularly titillated the community the time she had made the soul-cleansing confession at the Brush Arbor Tabernacle and in the sweet agony of repentance, forgetful of the congregation and their nasty hunger, telling her God what He must be told, had said, "O Father, I try to be a good woman, but the devil's got his holt on me. I try to keep my body chaste. But ever time I think I have wrastled down temptation, have got a little somewhere towards the purity of the flesh, that hired man of mine, ole Harmie Jenkins, just comes in and blows out the lantern and jumps in bed. And then I'm a goner, Lord, purely a goner. Cause the devil tempts me with what I got to have. And I don't know no way out of sinnin. I'm unworthy, God, and need to be whipped with a black-snake whip."

That was Mamma. And Harmie had married her and it was no longer a sin. Mamma was in her fifties. But her great hungers had never died. She could still eat more than a big man, and chop sprouts with an eye hoe along with the best hoe hand. Sam loved her and felt good in her presence.

After breakfast he went with Harmie and the children to do the chores, which under the circumstances were fun for everybody. Then the kids were gone to school and there was nothing to do all morning except sit and talk and fool with the fire.

Everybody felt the coming year would be a good one for farming. All this rain, despite the drought of the pre-ceding year, had put a good season in the ground. "The moistures," as Harmie said, "had met."

Of course Mamma and Harmie wanted to know the lat-est on Granny, and Sam was dying to tell them of the good leg-switching Nona had given her, but did not, for fear they might somehow misunderstand, though who should know better than they that Granny had long since passed the time when anything but child-reasons swayed her, that in her present condition anything but child-measures were wasted on her?

Then while they sat there and Sam passed his tobacco and papers to Harmie and invited him "to crank one up," Mamma began telling one of her kind of stories, how this young bride of ten months, who lived with her husband,

Tume Rutherford, in the post oaks, had thought Tume was deceiving her. For though she knew his hound was too sick to hunt, still he went hunting every night, leading the droopy dog into the woods on a string. A lone woman lived not far off, so when, on one of those nights that Tume was supposed to be hunting, his bride found the sick dog tied to a bush in the woods, she was convinced that her husband was using the dog and the pretense at hunting only as a blind for certain goings-on incompatible with the obligations of wedlock. Directly she went home, cut her heavy gold-plated wedding chain in two, and tamped a half of it in each side of a muzzle-loading shotgun. Then she sat down to wait for her husband. When Tume came home at daylight, she fired the left-hand barrel into his breast, and he died in writhing, bloody surprise.

But the strange part of it was that when she went outside to sit on the edge of the porch where she could use her toe on the trigger to shoot the other half of the chain into her own body, she found a heavy catch of varmints where her husband had dropped them in the yard. And the mystery of that catch had never been solved.

Harmie's comment was that he'd heard of people catching a lot of things in neighbor ladies' beds, but he had not known until now that possums and coons were on the list.

Mamma's more serious theory was that Tume, who had hunted since he was a baby and had always been successful with no matter what kind of old dog he might have, had possessed the ability to scent animal trails with his own nose. Moreover, she believed he could run those trails through the dark woods until the prey was finally driven up a tree and captured. Tume had, as she delicately stated her belief, whifflecated with no neighbor ladies whatever, had actually been hunting every night, but, afraid that his bride might be upset by the knowledge that he possessed canine powers, had dragged the sick dog along only as a mask for his own extraordinary but innocent abilities.

It was an idea, credible or not, which Sam found irresistibly fascinating as he sat there looking into the fire.

Later, there being two axes and Harmie having a cold, Sam went with Mamma to cut some wood and was beaten at it and proud of Mamma. Then, near dark, the wind lay and Sam ate a couple of buttered sweet potatoes, called the dogs, and went to the woods.

Now he was a tall man striding through the naked woods, which were clothed only with falling night, to hunt down the furred animals; following Zoonie and the cur, who were busily reading and editing the tangle of trails on the woods floor, disregarding the field-mice and rabbit trails, the bird tracks and those of the domestic stock that had wandered here, and the faint, lingering traces of squirrel musk.

The dogs were transfigured. They were no longer whiners after buttermilk or fire heat, were no longer slinkers or sluggards, but were roaming the dark woods with the strange dignity of things doing what they were born to do, of things afire with mastery and fierce intention.

Now Zoonie was chipping the brittle night to pieces with his small, fast, sharp bark, and Sam knew an animal was marooned in the night there above the little dog. It proved to be a possum, and as Sam climbed the blackjack tree, armored as it was with toothed bark, he was full of the hot flush of the chase and the haunting minor dissonance of sympathy that goes out to a thing that is alone and is doomed and that knows it.

Sam could not push it out on the ground because the dogs would slash it and ruin the fur. So with a stick and the light he toyed with the beast until it began to play dead. Once it began the pretense, Sam knew it would continue that all night.

Soon he climbed down the tree with it, holding onto its hairless tail, and fought off the dogs, though the cur was so fierce in his determination to get his teeth into the possum that Sam was for a moment afraid of him. Even so, Sam pretended not to be, and beat him away with a heavy stick.

When the dogs were launched again and Sam had walked two hundred yards, he heard a rattling in the leaves near by and went to it. Suddenly the light fell on a skunk, all shining black and white in the radiance of the lantern, perfectly confident that whatever manner of creature was approaching, that creature would know what would happen to him if he came any closer.

As Sam set the lantern down, the skunk, with thrilling poise, turned his stern to Sam and eyed him critically over his shoulder, sure of his weapon.

Sam was afraid that the slight but abrupt noise of cock-ing the gun would startle the skunk and launch him on his offensive of chemical warfare. But Sam also knew that in any conflict the worst thing of all is to be afraid. Firmly his right thumb drew back the hammer which would drive home the firing pin. At the resultant clicking sound, which seemed sharp and loud in the tense silence, a tremor ran over the skunk. Then through the notch in the rear sight and just above the lump of darkness which was the front sight, Sam could see the skunk's left eye, bright and calm. Slowly, so as not to spoil the aim, Sam's trigger finger closed, and in a single instant the skunk was a dead thing.

Where a moment ago it had been all loveliness and calm certain threat, it was now a lump of meat to be denuded with great care, to be robbed of its shining coat and left in nakedness to freeze and thaw and rot.

And now the dogs were barking somewhere off in the night, far ahead, to be reached before the quarry should run through the intermeshing treetops and escape. Sam picked up his things and began running to them.

When Sam came in next morning just at dawn, having taken a sight on the north star—which was the only one he knew definitely, since the two stars that form the front of the cup of the Big Dipper point outward toward it— he had the hides of seven possums, one skunk, one coon, and one ring-tail, and an amount of respect for Mamma's yellow cur that was Mamma-big. In the first place, to tree a ring-tail is not a sorry dog's job, and the coon, which had made his final stand on a log in the middle of a creek, had fought that yellow dog magnificently and shrewdly, had half drowned him several times. But the yellow dog had never yielded an inch, oblivious of everything except his driving desire to fight and kill, while Zoonie attacked from the rear, until Sam had been able to shoot the coon.

There had also been some pretense made at a fox race when the dogs happened on one, but he was out of their class when it came to speed and soon convinced them.

Now Sam was coming into the yard and the kids ran to meet him and he let them take his burdens. Mamma, who was standing in the kitchen door, said come tank up on breakfast and then get some sleep and she'd wake him up later for a big roast-possum dinner. Sam had brought home four, it being out of the question to carry more, and Mamma said she'd just roast them all and use the left-overs for sandwich meat for the kids.

After breakfast he got out of his clothes and went to bed, falling almost immediately into that exotic, delicious daytime sleep that waits for those who have hunted hard, who have not slept through, but lived through, the raw violence of the night.

Sam stayed at Mamma's six days, hunting all of every night, keeping the house flooded with fresh wild meat, and enjoying the tempo of a huntsman's life, with its single responsibility to hunt and catch, eating marvelously well, and being refreshed, moreover, by the different rhythms and flavors of a family not his own, enjoying his mother's long, emotional prayers, which rang through the house whenever she felt like praying.

But the weather, though cold, had been fair for four days and Sam was eager to get home and begin turning his ground. In farming he always tried to be forehanded in his work, knowing that by the time the weather and a hundred other impediments had finished delaying you, the job would be completed none too early. Besides, he wanted Ruston to understand that he was no sluggard, that he was ready to approach the making of this crop with his tail up and his stinger out.

So on the seventh day, which was a Thursday, Harmie hitched the team, and Mamma sacked up fifty pounds of sweet potatoes, a couple of pecks of dried black-eyed peas, and some peanuts for the children, which she pressed on Sam.

It had been a splendid week and Mamma kissed him so many times in parting that he and Harmie were both beginning to feel a little queer before they could get in the wagon and start off.

This was the second day of the fur season and Sam sold his pelts in town for twelve dollars. Out of this he bought Harmie two bottles of beer and sent Mamma and the kids a big two-bit sack of mixed candy. The rest he spent at the store for gingham and groceries, a pair of shoes for Daisy, a tablet and two pencils, snuff for Granny, and tobacco. He bought six dime cans. Then he caught a ride as far as the mail box, from where he signaled the family to come help carry.

9

NOW the time was come to do the long, toilsome
thing with the land. A coarse thing of aching muscles and
heavy tools. A dirty, sweaty arm drawn across the face,
stinking and burning and scratching, planting grit in the
eyes.

Hunting was over, and fishing must be subservient to
this commitment you were making to the land. It would
be a strange conflict where you alone of its participants
were visible. You would toil in bright light all alone, and
the flood gods and the drought gods would watch you,
ruminating and invisible, trying to ferret out what you
were hoping against, waiting very patiently for you to
weaken and tell them by begging them not to.

It wasn't fair, but there it was. You could not even take it or leave it. You had to take it and fight the thing out with work in the sun. Which was only half of it. But a big half. For both halves were big halves. Plump and packed. And the other half you did with your poor cunning and your guts, in what to you was the dark, though they could see in it as well as day. They had the ax on you, but you had a defense against them, a panacea that you knew would work—not flashily perhaps, but it would work. And that was such a simple thing. Just a kind of stubborn guts. Maybe it wasn't much, but there was no substitute for it. Once you really got your tail between your legs, you were a goner. And by goner you meant precisely: one of those who'd tried hard and folded up and were now, and their families with them, the kind of ugly, sickening joke which a group of beaten things becomes.

Like Whit Burnaby and his miserable yet ludicrous tribe in Hackberry.

If you worked like a son of a bitch and just barely got by, Hackberry looked on you as a peasant. Just exactly that, which is one of the least ridiculous things on earth.

Everywhere, and in Hackberry too, peasanthood means a hard life lived with simple fortitude. It also means a thing which outsiders can push only so far. A thing that is running in low gear but has stamina and is getting somewhere slowly. So you are persevering and indestructible, because you know that as long as you are you'll survive. You've got to hold a final rock of fierceness behind your back, with which to meet the still worse times that no one can promise won't come.

And when you are naked of that, you are Whit Burn-aby—a clownish slob.

Therefore you don't quit; no matter how rough it gets, you don't let fall that small final store of fierceness, but retreat into yourself, and armor yourself with apathy like a limber, impenetrable shell. You keep on digging, maybe whetting on the point, but digging, until you finally get some little old half-assed break.

What else can you do? You have to play the only way you're allowed to. Which is with the malicious gods looking down on you, and you, if you're simple enough, thinking you're just out in the field all by yourself except for the mules.

Perhaps that is what has got the best of Henry Devers.

In any case, now the hunting is over. The ancient commandment that existed a hundred centuries before there were ten, the one that says, "Kill and eat and live," has been obeyed. A few dregs of the blood of your forefathers, which still flows in your veins, have been set afire. An old hunger has been fed, the ancestral ritual observed.

And now it is time to do the thing with the earth, the thing that is still big and meaningful in your blood, because in yours, at least, time clocks, the factory whistle, the whir of machinery and stink of chemicals have, as yet, no place.

It is the twilight of your conflict, not with men or with beasts, but with the gods.

The dawn of this big, yearlong round.

And it is time to begin.

IO

THE land was crusted over, gray-black and ready, still too cold to germinate seed, but by no means too cold for breaking.

Ruston came and walked over it and crumbled a handful, like stale chocolate-cake crumbs, in his hand.

"It's just waiting on us," he said. "Let's see you do your stuff."

As they stood there, they had a feeling about each other. Though Ruston knew he ought to know better, he kept feeling that Sam had some stuff to do, and Sam felt that Ruston would keep out of his way.

Next day tools came. A cutter to chop last year's cotton stalks, which were bigger at their base than your thumb and tougher than seasoned willow. Long blades, the cutter was, fashioned into a cylinder that rolled against the dead stalks, pushing them over and cutting them. There was a rake for pulling the cut stalks to the end of the rows to be burnt, a sweep for center-furrowing, and a middle-buster for sundering the old rows, for lifting their bottom dirt to sun and light and air. Finally there were two great black mules named Weaver and Frisno Emma, and corn to feed them with.

But the cutting and raking, even the center-furrowing, were but preliminary things in which the mules coasted and the man rode. Not until this was done was it time for the main event, for ramming the great middle-buster into the old rows, which were knitted into a greater formidableness, into a kind of reinforced earthwork, by the forever down-going roots of last year's cotton. Into these he must drive the steel point, drive it down a foot into the row-ridge and plow, sunder earth, send the great clods tumbling stubbornly, but tumbling, out the rusty plow wings, which soon would be gleaming. He must guide the plow's snout evenly down the line it would be least inclined to go, breaking land.

Now farming had begun. The long, cumulative act of creation had begun, and not in the sand. Here something would come of it, something beautiful and substantial. And the nights were dead with sleeping, and the days, from edge to edge, were packed with labor, and there was no hiding from accomplishment. Each hour the bright, rough black area of new-plowed land grew larger, and that part of the land which was still unawakened decreased.

Your arms also told you you were getting the job done, especially in the shoulders, where the joints seemed to get shaken loose, and the small of your back, which the winter had softened, would keep thinking of going somewhere to lie down, and your legs were inhabited by shaft-like pains. The clods tried to bury your feet alive.

But the mules took it. You had the plow slammed in deep, but they were going on and you had to go too; you had hold of something you couldn't turn loose.

And as your legs grew more weary still, you were hammered by how much more there was to do, how many million steps were yet to be taken, how many thousand rocks and roots would send the plow, charged with mule strength, lurching off its course.

You combated these thoughts by thinking that when you really got hardened, it didn't matter how long the rows or days were. Once you really got in shape, you could plow to Kingdom Come and after the first couple of hours not get much tireder.

Sometimes it became necessary to play tricks on this animal you lived in. You treated it like a child. Or a drunk man uptown.

The first hour you didn't tell it anything, because it was doing all right. It was feeding on the decreasing stiffness in itself that a night's sleep had lodged there. During that first hour each step, each row, became more comfortable, more normal.

But nine o'clock thoughts were bad ones. They said you were still going downhill into the valley of the day. You hadn't done much of anything yet and you were already getting a little tired. You thought: If I had any sense I wouldn't be here. You thought about how much fun people had who worked in gangs. They weren't ever lonesome.

So you began pretending days didn't count, that dinner was the thing you were working toward. You ignored the afternoon and thought why, hell, the morning's over half finished. This was cheating because you'd started a little after seven, when good daylight came, yet you pretended you had started at six, like in big summer. And if you had begun to get hungry, you didn't have to pretend so hard that dinner was what you were aiming at, because you were. But those first few days with the middle-buster you weren't, because it was such a wild, surging thing, by the time you'd wrestled it all morning your guts were screwed up in such a knot that you weren't hungry.

But when noon finally came, and you unhitched and watered the mules and put them in the little mule pasture, you really felt like going home and sitting around and smoking, and maybe being tempted by a piece of hot bread and a few sirup.

And the babble of Granny was pleasant and lively with its fast-changing moods which might range from expansiveness through petulance to fury to an amusingly exaggerated but serious portrayal of martyrdom. You realized it was entertaining only because you were too tired to pay much attention and hadn't been hearing it

all morning. However, it took a little something out of
you to look at Nona's face. She had been listening all
morning, and Granny didn't pour off Nona's back like
she did off yours.

Lots of times listening to the old woman would be
really funny to you. For example, the time when she was
late getting to the table, which was so unlike her that you
made some remark about it, and she explained, "I taken a
dose of salts, Sammy boy, and slept right smack through
em. I just been out there wrenchin out these old drawers.
Person gets old, they haven't got such a good holt on
theirselves as when they're younger."

But Granny was a human, or almost one, and not the
thing that was frightening Sam and Nona. Granny, when
she became absolutely intolerable, could be switched.
This other matter wasn't so simple.

It was the thing that was happening to Jot that was
taking the sap out of them all. Other people might not
have noticed the difference in Nona, but Sam did, and
knew why it was there.

Hardly had the weather turned off fine, and the tools
come, when a little sore appeared in the corner of Jot's
mouth. In every other way he seemed healthy, but the
little sore came, and spread, just slowly and steadily, until
it was the size of his hand and was still spreading. All of
every day Nona had been watching it spread, knowing
there was no reason for it, that Jot had not been sick, but
that the sore had simply come and spread and was going
to possess him.

It was a thing that the gods had fastened on him before

your very eyes. The unknown was there in your house, and the way you recognized its presence was by seeing it devouring one of your babies.

Finally Nona said, "Sam, we got to get him to town and have him doctored."

A doctor, especially one of those who had let all your family that were dead die, was a trivial defender against the gods, but there was no other.

"I'll take him Sunday," Sam said. "I know it ain't hardly possible, but if you can, I'd try to keep his face and hands about half-way clean. We sure don't want no worms to get in him."

"All right," Nona said.

Sam made a cigarette and went back to the field.

II

EARLY Sunday morning, which was frosty, Sam left the house, carrying Jot on his shoulder. The baby was wrapped in the half-blanket left from Daisy's coat and was happy to be going somewhere with his father.

By nine o'clock, having caught a ride with some Mexicans after the first mile, Sam and Jot were in Dr. White's office.

Dr. White was an old man who still appeared to have the leathery, physical toughness of a ranch hand, and was always full of a kind of nervous impatience. He looked as if he had taken an uncommon amount of weatherbeating in his life, and could take a great deal more.

"Well, well . . ." the doctor said in a kind of detached

flurry which usually hovered about him, though it was plainly somewhat less than skin-deep.

He had followed Sam into the office, which was always left open. It was neither very dirty nor very clean, but you could get a leg set there, or get sewed up after a fight, or get your claps doctored. If you were going to have a baby, you had that at home.

"I sure hate to bother you, Doctor," Sam said. "I tried to get some of them others, but they wouldn't come downtown."

The old doctor smiled shortly but warmly at Sam. What Sam had said conveyed considerable information and respect: Sam had known Dr. White would come to anybody who was sick, and he also knew there would be no money in it for whoever treated Jot. He had tried to save Dr. White the trouble of coming downtown on a profitless journey. But it hadn't worked.

The other two doctors in the town were younger, more progressive, and had acquired most of the pay practice. They were trying to make a living and were succeeding, which was all right. But Dr. White seemed to think he was there to treat the sick, and that was what he did. You could look at his face and tell he was not a man who just did something for a fee.

The doctor didn't look at Jot. He looked at Sam. Just now, he didn't bother with Jot's temperature or pulse or when did his bowels move.

"You don't have a cow, do you, Sam?"

"No, sir."

"Well, you better get one."

"I ain't got no way to get one."

"Raise a heifer for somebody. Meantime, borrow milk. I don't care where you live, some neighbor will let you have enough for this child. At least a pint a day. Much better, a quart."

"All right, sir. And what medicine?"

"He don't need any medicine. What vegetables have you all been eating this winter?"

"Why, not any, hardly."

Sam didn't think it would be necessary to explain that vegetables didn't grow in the wintertime.

"You got any money at all?"

"Yes, sir; sixty cents."

Dr. White exhaled and looked at nothing out the window.

"Go spend it on some vegetables," he said. "Get some lemons and give the baby a glass of lemonade twice a day."

The nervous impatience returned to the old man and lifted him out of the chair.

"That's all," he said. "Let's go."

As they went down the stairs (the office was on the second floor, over the drug store) Sam recalled that his own middle name was White, after the doctor, and that that had been the only pay the old man had ever got for making the delivery at his birth.

"Let me know how he gets along," the doctor said mechanically, but meaning it, and left Sam at the bottom step before Sam could even thank him.

Then Sam remembered he hadn't asked the doctor how sick Jot was.

From the back of the drug store, Sam phoned Russell and told him his plight, and that he'd have to ask somebody to open a store to sell him a measly sixty cents' worth of vegetables.

"Would you feel like doin it, Russell?"

"Hell, yes. Wait on the corner."

Russell was another one of those nervous ones.

As he unlocked the store ten minutes later, he said, "Your folks aren't too high-toned to eat a few wilted vegetables, are they, Sam?"

"Course not."

"Then get that tow-sack and come on."

When the sack was filled with wilted cabbage and turnips and sprouting onions and soft bananas and shriveled lemons and the like, Russell put some garden seeds in a sack and said, "Now God damn it, Sam, go plant a garden. Here, put some of these seed potatoes in your sack."

"Gosh," Sam said when Russell refused the proffered sixty cents, "how come you to do this nice thing to me, Russell?"

Russell ran his fingers through his hair with a kind of tense helplessness.

"I don't know," he said. "Don't worry me about it. Come on and I'll haul you home."

Russell's car rattled because he went all over the county trying to collect bills and to trade for anything he thought he could make money on.

He was so energetically moody that when he didn't say something, it was hard for you to either. A mile out in the country, he broke the silence.

"Why don't you gripe?" he said baldly.

"I don't know," Sam said, mystified.

Russell went back into himself.

He put Sam out at home, turned the car with a kind of furiousness expressed not by his face but by the car, and left.

Late that afternoon Sam went over to the Hewitts', where he found the old man dressing a home-made ax handle with a rasp. Sam told him what the doctor had said, that somehow milk must be obtained for Jot.

"I haven't come beggin and I haven't come borrowin," Sam said. "If you could let me have a little pan o milk every day, I'd keep track of it like it was money, and work it out."

"I don't reckon we'd have any trouble about that," the old man said. "We got it for the chickens most of the time, anyway."

Sam squatted against the barn while the old man went on working.

"It may seem funny," Sam said, "me comin to you like this for milk when my next-door neighbor's got six cows and you ain't got but two, but we're already usin out of his well and he don't like that none too much."

"Glad you came to me," the old man said. "First place, he probably wouldn't of let you had it."

"What's wrong with that sucker?" Sam asked, perplexed.

"Sometimes I've wondered if maybe it ain't cause he ain't got no confidence in hisself nor nobody else," the old man said. "He's the worst scared feller of not gettin his share I ever saw. Lessen he gets about eight times the best of a trade, seems like he's scared to make it. I been knowin that boy a long time an I'm mighty fraid he's what you'd call a mean, jealous-hearted son of a bitch. I could be mistaken bout that . . . but I ain't."

"I give him a fish one day," Sam said, "and he just knowed he was gettin some kind of round-house friggin."

The old man put down his work and took a chew of tobacco.

"You had any experience with idiots?" he asked Sam.

"You mean about Henry?"

"Come on into the barn."

Sam followed him to a stall where there were a brown cow and a scrawny little calf. About both of them there was an air of melancholy resignation.

"That calf," the old man said, "ain't even got sense enough to suck. Ain't somethin done about it mighty quick, it's gonna die. If you want to undertake to raise it for me, take em both. If you raise that calf, you'll more'n repay me for what milk you get out of the cow. If you don't, I'm gonna knock it in the head. I ain't got time to be runnin no lunatic asylum for addle-headed calves."

Sam didn't say anything. He was too concerned with the problem before him. He slid the calf under the cow, held its mouth open with one hand and squirted a little milk into it with the other.

Once its gullet seemed to work half-heartedly.

"Its nose is goin to have to be helt," the old man said. "I never expected to see a livin creature with less git-up-an-go than Finley, but looks like that calf's got it."

Then Sam saw the old man was ashamed of himself for saying what he had, and Sam looked back at the calf and picked it up.

"I got plenty of pasture along the river for the cow," Sam said. "Just winter grass and rescue grass now, but enough o that to hold her. We'll keep the calf up at the house. One o these days it's liable to catch onto what its jaws is for. I guess ole Brownie'll follow us on over there."

"Sure she will," the old man said. "I reckon she likes the thing cause it's hern. I wish you luck on the calf."

"I sure thank you for the use of the cow. I know the kids'll make a heap over this here runty calf, and Nona too, for that."

When Sam came up to the house, the family was already in the yard, standing in awe before him and Brownie and the calf.

"That boy!" Granny exclaimed. "Was he to come waggin in one of these days with a bokinstrictor I wouldn't be one bit surprised."

While Sam milked Brownie and Zoonie barked at her, the children tied a bright rag around the calf's neck and named it Snookums. The cow they named Uncle Walter, after a favorite relative.

When Sam held the calf's nose to choke the warm milk down its throat, the others held their breaths.

The feeding was a success.

"Why, shuckins," Granny exclaimed, "all he needs is a little practice! Fore long he'll be a-eatin the very posties outen the fence."

Daisy ran in circles around Jot singing, "Snookums et! Snookum zet!"

And Jot got down on all fours and said to Daisy, "I'm Snookums. I'm Jot, Snookums calf."

Then Nona brought some cups and Sam filled them from the bucket and said, "Now let's see if y'all got more sense than that calf."

When Ruston came, there was no use for either him or Sam to say anything. The record of Sam's work was there, and no mistake could be read into it. It was good and there it was.

And when all the land lay turned, and the steel teeth of a harrow had shattered the clods into a broad sea of gray-black crumbles that were pleasing to the eye, Sam looked about him from the back of the homing mules and said, "We done all of that ourselves. Just kept a-hunchin and didn't let up." He rolled a cigarette, riding sideways. "And, by God, we done good. Fore too long now we'll be plantin corn, and long about the Twin Days, or maybe a little before, we'll plant cotton. Then we'll really have our crop a-goin."

As she walked away from the turned land, the finished

land, Frisno Emma broke wind thunderously, almost theatrically, and there was bravado and jauntiness in her manner, as if to say the three of them were equal to twice that task, and Sam slapped her neck and laughed and loved her.

12

AGAIN it rained and Sam and the mules rested. He sat and talked with the family, listened to Granny's endless chatter, and helped Nona in the impossible job of trying to keep Jot's face clean. Snookums, having no choice in the matter, was thriving. Uncle Walter was giving a gallon and a half of milk every day.

Sam discussed planting times with old man Hewitt. After all, it had thundered in February, which was supposed to be a sign that a frost would come in April. What did the old man think?

"I don't know," he said. "Seems foolish to go against the signs. I planted peas twice when the moon was in the flower and both times they just flowered big and never made any peas. Don't you go by the signs in fishin?"

"Maybe they ain't real signs exactly," Sam said, "but I know risin water is good, and fallin water bad, that moonlight nights are bad and dark ones are good. I don't really care for no east wind for that matter, or north ones either."

"They're signs, all right," the old man said. "In my little ole fishin I used to watch the stock grazin. If they grazed open and easy, good fishin. If they huddled in the woods, no taters."

"I'm a great hand to study bait," Sam said. "They's a season for tree buds and caterpillars and worms, and maybe it sounds funny, but I've done mighty good fishin under an ole overhanging vine full of ripe grapes with just them grapes for bait."

"Well, I've always figgered there might be something to signs," the old man said. "Figgered some feller must of watched close and then give out a sayin about the thing and if it worked, it stuck and people used it to go by. If it didn't work, I figger it'd play out."

"Sounds mighty reasonable, all right," Sam said, then clappy Finley came in and said to Sam, "Let's go set out some lines."

Which they did in the brown water, yet too cold, and caught but two fish for their trouble. However, they seined along the gravel bars and caught enough suckers in Sam's minnow seine to make a mess for both families.

It was while they were walking along the bank beside the long hole that they saw something that stopped their hearts beating. A catfish of the most gigantic proportions floated to the top for a moment, and then with a gentle, undulant motion of his great tail went back down.

They looked at each other.

"Why, that bugger was bigger than a hog!" Sam said. "His ole nose whiskers was the size of a lead pencil."

Marveling, they walked on home. The fish was bigger than any either of them had ever seen, a bigger fish than either of them had ever supposed might exist in the San Pedro.

And now in their little world there was a new being, an incredible monster, one to scheme against on sleepless nights. For to whoever caught Lead Pencil fame would be assured. His capture would make a legend that would be told whenever the San Pedro men sat around a fire at night waiting to run their lines. Whoever caught that fish would sell only the carcass. The feat of catching him would be non-transferable. Or if it happened when you had money, you could give a fish fry that would in itself make history.

Sam knew that now an issue had arisen between himself and Finley, a goal coveted by them both. But he also felt safe that, barring the greatest accident, old Lead Pencil the Fabulous would never be brought ashore by any such puerile creature as Fin.

They promised each other not to tell a soul about the presence of this monster in the long pool below the rapids.

At noon the next day, while Sam was drawing water at the well, Henry Devers came out.

"That your boat down in the big hole?" he asked.

"Sorter, I guess."

"How do you mean?" Henry asked.

"It come floatin down the river on that big rise."

"Then it tain't yours at all."

"I figger it is till its folks come for it."

"Done anything bout locatin em?"

"I told three or four there in town. It'll get around."

"You ort to of advertised it in the paper."

That was too ridiculous for comment. If you caught somebody's boat and pulled it ashore and started the word, how could they possibly expect more?

"Next time I'm in town," Henry said, "I'll tell Ferdy Whiff." (Ferdy was the constable.) "He'll be a big help in findin the owners."

Sam saw Henry watching his face to see if this suggested introduction of the law into the case would make him flinch.

"If I was you," Sam said, "I just wouldn't worry about it. They'll come get it fore long."

"Finley says there was a seine in the boat and you been usin it."

"That's right."

"What if it gets tore?"

"It just gets tore. Maybe I'll patch it and maybe I won't."

With any neighbor Sam would have tried to be patient. With this one, who held control of the family water supply, he had to be.

"Would you let it out on loan?" Henry asked, and Sam knew he was secretly proud of his question. It was one of those that could not be answered protectively. If you said yes, Henry would point out that you were taking unwarranted liberty with another man's property. If you said no, you'd seem ungrateful for the use of the well.

"Don't know," Sam said. "Need to figger on that."

For a minute Henry chewed a stick nervously.

"Tell you what I'll do," he said. "It ain't nothin to me, but just to show you my heart's in the right place, I'll furnish a dime on that two-bit ad. Costs a nickel a word. We'd say: 'Found boat on San Pedro.' Your name on it comes free."

Sam began to realize Henry had been brooding about the boat.

"No, sir," Sam said. "All I've done those boat folks is a kindness in saving their boat. I don't owe em no ad. I started the word and the word'll have to do."

"Now I think of it," Henry said, "you could do it free. Say: 'Found red boat on San Pedro River. Owner can have same if he will pay for this ad.' "

That son of a bitch was getting on Sam's nerves. Gradually he was maneuvering Sam to a spot in which Sam would have to admit that he wanted the use of the foundling boat during whatever interval was required for the word to get around. Sam had squared things with his conscience and now Henry was trying to force a kind of shame on him. Either that or deprive him of what Sam considered a bit of earned use of the boat.

Suddenly Sam thought of something.

"I got to find Finley today. Ain't seen him around, have you?"

"Not since last night," Henry said. "You can count on

me to tell Ferdy Whiff. He'll be glad to help you find the right folks."

Not since last night. . . .

So that flappy-mouthed Clappy had been with Henry last night telling him about Lead Pencil, and Henry was trying to get rid of the boat at once, before it could be used in fishing for the big fish. If Henry was going to fish from the bank, he wanted you to also, despite the fact that both the boat and Lead Pencil were your own discoveries. Flappy Fin had told their secret for a mess of momentary awe.

"I got to go," Sam said. "Nona's waiting for her water."

And he went, his body down the footpath and his thoughts down the vast avenue of the future which was inhabited with great intuitive decisions concerning Jack-and-the-Beanstalk crops; and a monster living his days beneath hollow banks and his nights on the prowl in the black water; and days of incredible accomplishment with plow and hoe; and, for the time, security from the niggardly insults of absent pennies. Crawling with futile puerility along the edge of this grandeur would be clappy Fin and Henry Devers, while he himself and old man Hewitt were getting long-legged jobs done that would in the aggregate produce a thing of substantial beauty: the deeply satisfying thing that must come rhythmically at the end of the land cycle. In the fall, then, you'd be able to look at the result of your year's work spread out before you and to see what kind of man you were, unless some plague of weather or insects had broken the mirror.

"Well," Granny said when he came in, "I figgered you'd

jumped in the well, from how long you was gone, and us all over here hog hungry, waitin to start eatin."

"I was talkin to Henry."

"He's nice," Granny said. "He's got some sense. Says nobody preciates their ole folks till they're dead and gone, and then it's too late. Says come over just any ole time and have another good pow-wow. Says it's funny how a lot of folks think they can put stuff over on ole folks, when they ain't even comin close. Says his folks don't half preciate him, either, an him a-slavin his guts out for em year in and year out. Says gratitude is one of the easiest things they is to find, so long as you ain't lookin for it nowhere but in the dictionary; and if any in-law chilren of hisn ever lays a mesquite limb to *his* butt, somebody is gonna get a hole shot in em that no patch won't reach acrost."

"Dinner," Nona said.

They sat down to peppered beans with lard and garlic in them, and they were strengthening and good. And as Sam sat there eating, a strange, shocking notion came to him from nowhere.

I love Nona, he realized; and not for just what work I c'n get out of her.

For a moment he tried to think what life would be like with her gone, but hid from the black picture before actually visualizing it. While his jaws chewed, he sat there thinking about his feeling for her, comprehending that his love for her was so stable that it was almost transparent and neutral, like an extra dermal covering of cellophane that you hardly ever noticed; but it was there and tough and gave a dull, however slight, positive glow to her aspect in his eyes.

And he wished it were summer, that Nona were entirely clean, free of dirt and the smell of drudgery, and if not so soft a thing as feminine, at least completely womanish, scrubbed and forgetful of unending labor, and he might take her in his arms on a clean bed of blue clover beside the river.

But the winter was not yet entirely over, so he ate his beans and pleasantly did not hear the babbling of the old woman.

13

SAM was late getting his corn land seeded, and he
didn't like it. He had had to wait until the ground was
dry enough. When the hillside was ready, he began planting there in a little patch which Ruston said had got in
the habit of "dying" cotton. On land such as that, cotton
just dies in patches for no apparent reason except that
the land has been enfeebled by the gluttonous roots of
twenty consecutive cotton crops. So they would plant
corn there to get the use of the land, though Sam never
liked to grow corn on a hillside. He preferred the flats
where the ordinarily scarce rain would soak in instead
of running off. Especially when you were late getting
started. At best you had to crowd corn like hell to get it
made before the dry weather set in.

Sam was disquieted by remembering that it had thundered in February. But then if it was going to frost in April, it was going to and you hadn't any way to stop it. At least the corn would already be well rooted, and if the tops got cut down by frost, they would come out again. The crop would be delayed, but that, too, could not be helped.

Part of the land was going to be left idle under government subsidy. The rule was that it had either to lie idle or be planted in a non-commercial crop. And on this part Ruston had said Nona could plant her garden. She was up there now setting out onion plants, being watched by Granny, Jot, and Zoonie.

Over at the Hewitts', Sam could see the old man out working on his fence. He couldn't start planting yet because his land was all flat. Clappy Fin was not in sight. Probably home playing his Mamma some dominoes.

Then Sam saw Henry Devers come into his own field, which was also flat, and begin planting, and for a long time Sam couldn't make it out. That land was too wet.

Finally with a little shock of understanding Sam asked himself: "You reckon that rascal is out there plantin that mud just to keep from bein got ahead of?"

He could think of no other explanation.

Because the corn was late in the planting, it was time, when this was done, to plant the cotton. The earth was warm and it was time. The Twin Days were at hand. The signs were right and Sam's intuition said go ahead.

"This ain't any half-and-half cotton," Ruston said when

he brought the seed. "I'm burnt out on that. I used to think it was something to get a yield of as much lint as seed, but that don't pay. Staple is what you've got to have. This stuff makes less lint, but is supposed to make a fifteen-sixteenths staple."

So Sam planted it, and an overflow came and washed some of it away, and the standing water rotted some of what was left. But he replanted the inundated land, telling himself he was doing it at six bits a day, that the weather gods were giving Ruston a working over, not him.

It was near the end of this replanting that Sam went one evening after work to fetch Uncle Walter. He had left her tied near the river where there was a patch of bright blue-green rescue grass, so called because it grew thick and flourishingly before the other varieties came out in the spring.

But when he got there, she was gone. The branch to which she had been tied had been ripped away. He was annoyed. Now he would be late for supper. When he was tired in the first place, he'd have to search for that truant milk cow.

An hour later he had ceased to be annoyed; he was frightened. The moon was full and had come up as the sun went down. On through the brush he went.

It did not help matters that this was the season when the snakes, ordinarily willing to run out of your path, were blind. Or so reputed. Sam had always thought they were defending their eggs or their young. Whatever the reason, if you came near one, he nailed you.

But that was something that couldn't be helped. If one popped you, he popped you. You had to find that vanished cow.

He heard something moving heavily behind him, and he almost dared to hope.

"It's me," Nona said. "I came to see what was keepin you."

"The cow's gone," Sam said. "I've looked all over this side of the river."

"Maybe we better cross over, then," Nona said. "She could have."

"I just never much figgered she would," Sam said, "but we can try it."

They waded the river at a fast gravel shoal and began searching the woods, holding their minds focused on hunting, not daring to contemplate the thought that she might be gone forever—that somebody might have stolen her, led her to a truck and carried her away, or that she might have drowned in the river. She was their food, Jot's medicine, a trust on old man Hewitt's part that was holy if one ever was.

Already Sam could almost hear the wails of the children when they found out. What if the old man thought they had sold her?

Before long they came out on a wild-clover meadow. The moon lighted it with a bright blue-yellow glow, but there was no sign of a cow feeding.

"What's that over there?" Nona asked, pointing to an oblong mass on the meadow.

Sam saw it too, and a feeling of utter despair passed

over him. It was the cow. She was down, her legs sticking out starkly.

When they got to her, they saw her belly was swelled to twice its normal size. Sam felt her nose.

"She's still breathin," he said. "Just barely. She's bloated like hell. Probably been that way all day from eatin dew-wet clover."

"You better run for the old man," Nona said. "He'll know what to do."

"There ain't time, Honey. She ain't goin to live but just a minute."

"You know what to do?"

"Yes. An I'm gonna do it."

And Nona knew he was lying, that he was going to do something, but that he was not sure of himself.

"She's got to be stuck," Sam said.

Which was true. But how? He had never stuck a bloated cow or seen it done.

For a moment he waited, strainingly remembering the dozens of times he had butchered for other people, trying to place in his memory the exact location of the stomach, the point of entry for the knife where it would sever no intestine. He couldn't be sure, but he could wait no longer.

Nona shut her eyes.

"God," she said silently, "she's all we got in this world. Save er, God." Tears were running down Nona's face. "Take me if You got to take, but save the cow. They got to have her. She gives milk."

Sam opened his knife, held the long blade over a spot some five inches forward and down from the point of the hip bone, and, in terror lest he drive it through a kidney or some other vital organ, rammed it in. The tough hide resisted, but with his full weight he drove it in.

And the vile-smelling gas came rushing out under enormous pressure. A little blood. Not much. But a fog of stinking gas. You could see the distended stomach grow smaller like a punctured tire.

For a long time Sam and Nona stood there watching. Then Sam went around and scratched the cow's muzzle gently with his fingers.

"Uncle Walt," he said, "nobody but us'll ever know how much pressure we had on us, or how nice it is to get it off."

Before long they had her on her feet, and were experiencing the great joy of leading her back, slowly, tenderly, to the pole-pen Sam had built for her beside the river.

Next day when Sam told old man Hewitt, the old man said, "That was a close call, all right. Knowed a feller once found all eight of his cows bloated like that and had come off from the house thout his knife. Didn't have a thing to do nothin with but a .22 gun, so he just shot the last frazzlin one through the belly. And he didn't lose a cow."

By now the corn was up and the Johnson grass came up among it, masquerading as corn. With a sweep Sam plowed it out of the middles, and with hoes he and Nona chopped out the rest, at the same time thinning the stalks.

The work was hard, but what was worse was that no power they could muster was great enough to keep Granny from trying to be helpful and cook something while they were away in the field. She regarded this as her season of usefulness, and nobody was going to stop her. If she'd just waited and let Nona fry something when she came in from work, it would have been all right. But each noon there was some boiled mess, either half raw or burnt, or with too much salt or sugar in it. And if you tried to curb her good, but devastating, intentions she had a tantrum.

"I'm just tard o bustin myself open tryin to please folks around here. Harder you work, more abuse you get. Oh, I know some folks lives too long and gets in the way. And their kindred expects em just to go sit off in a corner and never move nor say nothin and be a prisoner to theirselves. Try to fix somethin sides that eternal fried sow belly which ole folks' guts can't hannel, and get chewed up alive. Tard, I said, and ain't gonna take no more. Just gonna . . . gonna *do* somethin, that's what. An maybe when you look in on my cold dead face in that ole county pine box, you'll realize how much I done. How I've wore out my life in the service of others. And how scrubby I got treated by my own family."

"Granny," Sam said, "I've heard how you used to tell Granpa that all the time, about how he'd feel when he looked on your cold dead face, and he'd say, 'You keep on promisin, Edna, but don't never deliver the goods.'"

Like a wounded stag she eyed him, then walked deliberately over and put her hand on his chest.

"What's the matter, Granny?"

"You've got no heart," she said. "I knowed it. What keeps your blood a-circalatin I can't tell."

And then back to the fields, where the corn seemed to have grown while you were gone.

With both of them working, there is a dollar twenty-five coming in every day. And house rent. And Daisy doing well at school. And a fish or two off the lines nearly every morning, the fish trap having been long ago, and not without satisfaction, destroyed. Just keep your lines in the water and, for ammunition, a canful of big black-land worms a foot long that you pick up behind the plow.

Nona even has a pair of women's shoes. A dollar and a quarter they cost; a man-day and a woman-day spent in conflict with the Johnson grass. Now, thanks to the fact that flour and meal are available in sacks made of bright printed cloth, with the brand name stamped on only in water color, she has made some of these into a dress for herself. It is not anything fancy, because Nona is not an artist at designing dresses, but it is neither ragged nor, for the moment, faded, and will do. And since she has a change from the old overalls that have covered her until now, one of these days she'll be able to go to town of a Saturday.

But one thing is wrong, really wrong, and is getting your goat: what's happening to Jot. He's not getting any better. You've taken him back to the doctor and the doctor said the same thing: feed him right.

"But we hustled a cow to keep, Doc, and got a garden goin and he ain't gettin no better."

And that haunted look came in the old doctor's eyes, and he talked the calmest you ever heard him, and said, "Sam, don't you know I'd work a miracle for this baby if I could? Think of the thousands of times I've watched . . ."

But that was all. He didn't say any more. And you brought Jot home, silently, because if you talked to him these days he cried. He couldn't even stand for anybody to say nice things to him, to try to tell him little tales about how you were going to catch him some rabbits to raise. The sores on his mouth had not gone away. Patches of blue-purple were coming on his skin: one on his left forearm, one on his back, one on his foot. He was growing thin.

"Pore little feller," Sam thought. "Ain't done a thing. An yet this has come on him. Maybe I done somethin."

Spring sickness, such as Jot had, was not a new thing to Sam. It had made its appearance in his parents' family many times, and two of his relatives had died with it. Other people had other names for it, but the Tuckers called it spring sickness because your skin always broke out with it in the spring. Not without some surprise, Sam had heard Dr. White prescribe fresh vegetables for Jot, because it had always been assumed in his family that spring garden vegetables were one of its causes, since the appearance of both the vegetables and the disease was more or less concurrent.

"You reckon he ain't mistaken about what Jot ought to eat?" Nona asked.

"I don't know, Honey," Sam said. "I just don't know. We got to take as good care as we can of him, an hope for the best."

14

WHEN the corn had been hoed and it was still too soon to do anything to the cotton, Sam said, "Somethin's been a-worryin me kinda and I just now decided what it was."

Nona looked up at him silently, patiently, waiting to be told.

"Why, it's dewberry time in the sand hills," he said. "I been feelin em get ripe in the back o my mind. We got a few days now. Reckon we ought to go a-pickin?"

"What about the baby?"

"I sort of figgered on us all goin down to your daddy's maybe. You ain't seen im in a coon's age and there's not no better wild berries anywhere. Jot could stay at the house."

"Me an him," Granny said. "I'll run the cookin."

"Oh, you'll want to help pick," Sam said. "Be fun. You an Daisy can run a pickin race."

"I ain't mixin and minglin with no copperhead snakes," Granny said. "I'm already wearin one crooked toe them buggers ruint."

However, when Sam told her she might keep her berries separate and spend their entire proceeds on snuff, she agreed to pick.

When Friday afternoon came, the family kept their date with Daisy at the railroad crossing where she was to go straight from school, and they all started walking south down the highway. Sam was carrying Jot, Nona a bushel basket with a five-pound sack of two-cent yellow meal in it. Granny, bonneted, complaining of her feet, was carrying an empty gallon sirup bucket in each hand, with which she tried to wave down the passing cars, yelling, "Hold on there, feller! We got a long way to go. N I'm seventy years old and then some." Then as the car would whiz by, she'd yell, "Well, go on, you scalawag! Didn't want to ride in no cheap-johnny car nohow."

Walking on, disgruntled, her pride now hurt by this lordly indifference to her request as much as the pavement was hurting her feet, she'd turn to Sam and say, "It's a mighty funny bunch, it looks like to me, that the Lord seen fit to furnish with cars. Just skin right by you thout so much as a kiss-my-foot."

"Yes'm," Sam said.

Another car was coming. Once more the sirup buckets were flying.

Finally a man in a wagon with no seat in it gave them

a lift and by six o'clock they were standing off the dogs
in front of Corinth Macey's house.

Old Corinth, whose name derived from the town of
his birth in Mississippi, came to the door, saw the bayed
Tucker family in front of the house, and said, "Well, for
the land's sakes!" To the dogs he called, "Hush yo fuss.
Shame o yourseffs."

As the family streamed up on the front porch of the
ancient, paintless, leaning house, Corinth made no especial
effort to conceal his amazement at this visitation. He was
neither more nor less cordial than he would have been to
a meteor that had fallen in the front yard. However, as
Granny came up the steps, a soft little sigh of despair
did escape him. Corinth was, always had been, and always would be, utterly baffled and intimidated by this
old woman; so thoroughly, in fact, that his attempt to
hide it was futile. In Granny's estimation, and this was no
secret either, Corinth was white trash. Whenever they
were together, she comported herself like a princess in the
presence of a privy-cleaner.

But just now she smiled on him with generous, friendly
condescension and said, "Hello, Corinth. Run get me a
glass of cool water. I'm tard and hot."

A little miserably Corinth got it and came back, the
bewilderment on his face gently asking that it be removed
by some explanation.

"We came a-berry-pickin," Sam said. "Just till Monday. We brought our own meal."

That at last was something definite. Corinth looked a
little more relaxed.

"Set, everybody," he said, himself sitting (largely at the direction of his shriveling ego) on the floor, though there were chairs and stools enough for all the grown-ups.

Sam had put Jot on the bed, where he lay quietly, gently running his fingers through Zoonie's white hair, looking with a quiet blankness into Zoonie's eyes.

"There's some boiled armadillo meat on the back of the stove," Corinth said humbly, thinking of the old woman and dropping his eyes.

"Oh, is that so?" Granny said with amused haughtiness. "I was hopin we'd find some nice fried house cat."

"You ain't goin to get nothin but some peach-tree tea if you ain't careful," Sam said, confident of the deflationary value of this allusion to the switching Nona had given her.

"Well," Granny said disgustedly, "it's got so it's all a feller's life is worth to crack a little joke any more. I don't mind eatin a dab of armadillo, long as it ain't still got the shuck on it."

"What's wrong with the boy?" Corinth asked.

Sam told him.

"He'll get all right," Corinth said. "Had it about twenty times myself. How's things up on the river?"

He was glad to turn the attention away from himself. In most little gatherings of friends and relatives Corinth was quiet but not uncomfortable. His present uneasiness was just the effect this particular old woman had on him.

Corinth's own wife had long since died of a scratch on her arm that had developed into lockjaw. Now he

lived in this house which had been abandoned by its owners and their tenants. It sat on a sterile, weed-grown,
sandy-land farm in a neighborhood that was full of them.
On the hills the shallow top-soil had washed entirely away,
leaving only the clay subsoil and a scattering of ironstone
rocks. It was land that had made a few good crops in the
late 1800's, immediately after it was cleared. But these
crops had soon devoured the land's unstable capital of
humus and left it, depleted, to wash away. Even as pasture it was almost entirely worthless. These days it was
possessed only by Corinth and the quail and the jack-
rabbits, its narrow branch bottoms choked by wild vines
and bushes.

Corinth, now fifty-eight, blind in one eye by reason of
a cataract, listless, possessing not a single gram of initiative, subsisted on home relief. He had all of every day
to visit his neighbors or loaf in town or doctor his rheumatism. To a degree that startled him whenever he stopped
to think of it, he was a happy man; so much so that he
often wore a miserable expression to conceal his own
inner serenity from a world that seemed to resent too
much happiness in any of its people, and particularly those
who lived at public expense.

After a supper of bread and oven-browned armadillo,
which had all the tender succulence of a plump young pig,
he told his guests a piece of news.

The preceding week he'd spent the night in town, having remained at the domino hall until there was no chance
of catching a ride home. He had therefore been obliged
to sleep in the depot, but the benches were so uncom-

fortable that he had not been able to stay there after day broke.

He had hardly left the depot when he heard something come tearing down the street. The morning was still dark blue with left-over night, but in a moment the fast-moving object came close enough to see.

It was Morry Patterson, a second cousin of Harmie Jenkins, who had a notorious way with women.

"So then I seen it was Morry," Corinth said, "whizzin down the street barefooted, with his head throwed back and a shoe in each hand. And then he was gone. Bzzzt! Just like that."

The precise nature of the causes for this act and the personalities involved held their attention until bedtime.

Sunrise next morning found them in the woods—all but Jot and Corinth, who said his rheumatism had flared up slightly and that he'd stay at the house and look after the baby.

The berries on the ditch banks, decorated with sunlight and dew, shone like black-purple glass, except those that were not ripe, and they were jade and coral. Some of the vines were loaded with incredible stores of big, fat, ripe berries. On all the vines there were thousands of tiny thorns that slowly made your fingers smart worse and worse. Where the vines lay thickest, you lifted the whole mass gently with a stick to see if there were any snakes underneath waiting for the flies that the sweet, oozing juice of the berries would attract.

Since Daisy kept ahead of the rest and her sharp eyes found the best vines, Granny watched her like a quail hunter watching his dog. Then when Daisy commenced to pick, the old woman would horn in on Daisy's discovery and get herself sassed infuriatingly, and her feelings hurt. When Sam had adjudicated that dispute, Daisy would go on ahead, make another rich find, and it was all to do over again, until Daisy killed a little snake and kept it as a weapon to dangle at the old woman and put her into screaming, skirt-raising flight.

To Sam the evenings here at his father-in-law's were splendid. It was hard to be anything but content after a supper of dewberry cobbler when you were sitting on an old front porch in the sand hills. Especially after Granny had gone to bed and you knew there would be no further allusions to grown men who had calluses only on their behinds, or childishly heartless witticisms about people who were blind in one eye and couldn't see out of the other. The evenings were delightful because there was, in the long run, no better company anywhere than Corinth.

Not only was no current neighborhood gossip a secret to him, but he was a man to whom the old times were invariably luminous. Its legends, to him, were not subject to tarnish. He was not a man who lived by the hour or the day or, any more, by the season. Corinth's units were lifetimes. The quality of his patience acted upon and dispelled your own irritations of the present.

Corinth's deathless hero was Fayette Tucker, Granny's late husband and Sam's grandfather. Fayette was a man who had met not only life in general but Granny on their own terms, given them both cards and spades and a superb

beating. Or so, at least, Corinth chose to regard the out-
come of Fayette's conflict with these forces. For old Fayette had been Corinth's *alter ego*, had performed the dra-
matic actions of the non-physical Corinth that existed only
in fancy, but which in fancy raised what Corinth called
"unshirted hell."

"Remember like it was yesterday," Corinth said quietly,
drifting involuntarily and with grace into the past. "I was
comin into town on horseback late one Saturday afternoon and seen this drove of wagons and buggies and stuff
comin down the road. Thought, 'Funny it's such a big
funeral an I ain't heard of it.' But I couldn't make out no
hearse. All these wagons and things—I reckon fifteen. An
then they met me, and Buddy Cruikshank was in front
an says, 'You might just as well turn an go back,' an I
says, 'How come?' And he says, 'Ole Fayette's comin
home drunk from town, an got a shotgun cross his saddle bows an's makin everbody turn back the way they
come from, an's a-herdin em down the road.' So I just
turnt an joined the bunch and come on back to the house."

Corinth also recalled the time Granny had tried to lead
her husband to salvation, and how every time the preacher
came, Fayette would grab his gun and run under the
house, swearing that rather than accept salvation, he'd
gladly die, and so would the preacher if he made one false
move.

Even more fabulous was the time when Granny had
moved down the river to her parents' place and instituted
divorce proceedings. She had won and was threatening to
sue for the furniture when Fayette shipped it to her, as

he phrased it on a postcard, by water. He'd just hauled it as far as the bridge, thrown it in, and left its fate in transit and its ultimate safe delivery up to "Edna's friend, God."

"Not a time," Corinth said, "durin their whole married life did she make anything off of Mr. Fayette. He never conquered her, but she'd shore'n hell met her match."

Sam told about one of his childhood visits to his grandparents when the old man, though sober, had been nagged beyond his endurance. It was always a point of pride with his grandfather, and an advertised one, that he had never laid hands on Edna. On this occasion, however, as a substitute, he had picked up the four corners of the tablecloth on which their noon meal was set and thrown the whole thing out the window.

"Oh, he was fierce, all right," Corinth said, smiling with dreamy admiration at the memory of his idol. "A real ringtailed tooter, if there ever was one."

And though Sam had always been aware of the childishness of the old man's tantrums, he knew they were extenuated by a degree of exasperation that nobody who had not lived with Granny could ever have known.

Thus, in gentle, ever-lively reminiscence, on excursions into the past that Sam could not have made with his black-land neighbors, the evenings at Corinth's slipped away.

Ten o'clock on Monday morning found the Tuckers back in town. Sam sent Daisy on to school and left Granny and Nona and Jot in the shade of a tree by a culvert. He would have liked for Nona to go with him on his berry-peddling tour, but neither of them was willing to leave the child in Granny's care.

When Sam rejoined them at one o'clock, he brought with him a dime's worth of sliced boloney, a large onion, and a loaf of bread. He also brought enough lemons and sugar to make lemonade for the baby for ten days to come. To Granny, he gave a big brown bottle of Five Dot Garrett snuff. Then he handed Nona a light, flimsy little package.

"What's that?" she asked.

"Open it," he said.

When she did, she found a pair of shiny tan rayon stockings, which glistened in the sun. Granny's mouth puckered in disapproval.

"They're to go with your shoes and that dress you made," Sam said.

For a long time, standing there on the edge of the culvert, Nona looked at these adornments for her own body. Not necessities, mind you, but luxuries. Exotic, feminine luxuries.

Finally, feeling humiliated by her unimportance in this scene, Granny said irritably, "Well, ain't you goin to say your manners?"

"I don't hardly know how to," Nona said, blushing, starting off toward home, carefully re-wrapping the stockings so that the slick green paper would have the same folds that it had before. Once she looked at Sam timidly, then dropped her eyes, feeling tongue-tied and confused. She did manage to blurt out, "They're pretty."

Just then a man drove up in an empty farm truck, looked them over casually, and drove slowly on.

This was too much for Granny. She threw a bucket at him, but it only landed harmlessly in the truck bed, in which it passed on down the road.

"Well, I'll be jiggered!" she exclaimed, feeling swindled. Then, turning to Sam, she said, "This here's the last trip I'm ever takin. Folks on the road don't behave no better than them at home. I'm just goin back to the house and set and wait for my call to Glory."

15

By the time Sam had plowed a little dirt against his corn stalks, which the wind had loosened somewhat, the cotton had come up like long neat rows of blue, double, coat buttons, and it was soon time to chop it. He and Nona began at the first of the long rows.

Through the warming days chopping. Sending the blade slicing through the dark, hilled crumbles of earth. Killing weeds. Thinning cotton. Up, down, swing the hoe into a sort of limbo, a Nirvana, in which only a few muscles remain aware, and they not sharply. Sweat-wet clothes dragging coolly, coolly galling. And time no longer exists in minutes and hours, but in rows and acres. And even this is vague. A sea of up and down. Of bad

meals. A back that aches in your sleep. The savage growth
of the black land is in the weeds and you are chopping
them down. With the small of your back. In the chopping
trance all day for seventy-five cents, and you come out
of the fields at night having made it. But you feel all right
because you have done a good thing to the crop. Anybody
can earn six bits. But you have been chopping cotton,
have been doing something that in the long run makes big
sense. It's Ruston's owning, but it's your crop. Yours and
Nona's and Weaver's and Frisno Emma's.

It's lookin good, too, gettin somewhere. Maybe you
ain't, but it is. And it matters. It don't take any brains to
know that. You know you ain't just messin around, but
makin a crop. This is the one you're always goin to remember. The one where you really squirted your putty.
Not half-and-halfin and havin to skimp on this, and figger
close on that, or holdin up a plow in your hands all day
long to save two sorry mules from droppin dead. And the
weather havin no real holt on your somethin t'eat. Or
worryin your guts out. You're kind of straightenin up
once in your life and just goin after a crop in a nice long
swingin gait. Rest for Nona, like as not, this choppin, to
get away from the old woman. Done lived forever and
ain't gonna die till she gets good and ready. Old and tough,
like Lead Pencil. Just layin there under some hollow bank
soakin up the last fish he'd caught. Say a two-pound cat.
Just layin there digestin him and when the meat's all gone,
puke up the bones and lay for another one. Got to study
that big drift at the head of the hole. And beat Henry
there with the right bait when he's bitin. Says we'll take

time about on the well rope. . . . Time about, when it's done wore out. And worryin about that boat. Don't want you to have nothin he ain't got. And he's got forty times more stuff than me. Teams of his own, and tools. Always frettin about. When I ain't.

Where'll I be five years from now? Hoein, I guess, like now. And ten years. And twenty. Be up in my fifties then. A-hoein. Fifteen more fore pension time. Be draggin pretty slow by then. And the kids grown and got kids of their own. If Jot makes it. He's gonna. He's got to. And his very own kids, after he's got well and growed up and bred em, sayin Granpa's a goofy ole poot, but he ain't so bad. Says he don't do a blessed thing no more sides fool around the creek an collect his pension. He don't hoe no God damn cotton. Just sets on his can watchin for squirrels and fishin buffalo and a-fussin at us kids. An Granma gets hern too, cept she don't say much. Says it seems like she's kind of got tired. . . .

If it ain't a arrowhead right there in the furrow. Some Indian. A hunderd years ago. Made em dribblin water on hot rocks. This'n might of run through a man or a big buck deer. Indians camped here by the San Pedro. Summertime. "We won't even bother to put up the tents on this pretty night. Some of you boys go shoot some supper. I got to fix me up some new arrowheads. Ole Medicine Man, go boil up some roots and cure my son. Else we won't be happy on this nice river." An they never fretted with no cotton. N I'd of done better then. Been a pretty big shot. Cause I understand their kind of things. But now our sort of folks, the Indian sort that knows the woods and the weather, just fiddles with the land cause the money's gone out of farms, and factory folks don't want em. Can't do nothin else, go farm.

Land just catches the culls that can't do no good in cities. Cept me. I wasn't culled here. I blong. But there's too much cotton and too much corn. Ain't no secret from nobody. We go on raisin it cause it's all we know. Ain't worth enough in money to keep us alive, but the government's a-doin for us what it done for the arrow-makers. When their kind of work got useless an in the way. Farms ain't farms no more; not no real business. Just reservations where the government gives men money to stay there and keep off the relief. Reservations to stay on and raise somethin that you and the government plays like there's some use for. An it seems strange when you know this year's cotton'll be just as good, just as white, an a better staple than it ever was; just as much work to raise. Except there ain't no use for but about half of it. Ain't nobody's fault, I guess, but ourn for raisin cotton. More of us got to crowd into the factories, looks like.

Had a taste o that, all right. Time I done that scabbin in the Houston strike. Time they gathered up a bunch of us ole farm boys. And all the fun of meetin an startin off and they said they'd protect us, and all that money. Thinkin about it ridin, and how it would be to look at and walk around in a real ship, unloadin it, and all that money. And ridin down there in the truck, we all said what sonsabitches strikers were. Us boys said. Cause we needed to get mad to keep from bein ashamed. Maybe didn't even know we was wantin to, but needed it an

kinda did. And them kinds of fancy sonsabitches the pick-
ets called us, and we called back. But not as blisterin,
somehow.

And all them ten days it fretted me and I said I got a
wife an kid to feed, an no other way. All that money.
What if it is somebody else's job? Hidin in that God
damned warehouse day an night. Like somethin shamed.
Cause we was. And it kept gettin clearer. They're payin
me all this money to be wrong. Don't matter which side
of the strike is right or wrong. I know I'm wrong; dartin
in like a buzzard to grab somebody's job when the fight
starts. I'm such a flabby-tail I can't feed my folks bein
right. I got to take money for bein wrong. For goin
against my kind. That little ole shirt-tail full of hold-
your-head-up I always had ain't here no more. Folks can
look down on Sam Tucker an be right, and I said frig it
an quit. . . .

Them tough babies waitin at the gate, and I said, I
know you guys are layin for me, so I just came to tell you
I ain't on the scab side no more. I ain't been since I came,
but it just now got the best of me. An they says we ought
to break your God damned neck, and was goin to, only
a policeman came up and I said, please get me out of here
all in one piece.

Twenty-six dollars in one week. Near forty-five in all.
Take five weeks this way.

See no use of all them strikes, all that hell-raisin in the
first place. Why don't them buggers sit down and figger
what's fair for all an then go to work? Somethin's bound
to be fair for all of em. But they're so busy hatin each

other's guts, ain't thought about that. Don't neither side
want what's fair, but all they can prize out of the other
one. An yet, when you go to the factory, you got to take
sides, got to fight for what's unreasonable. Just a God
damned nightmare is all it is. Maybe one o these days
they'll get tired o actin like greedy little boys. Maybe
they'll get tired o friggin things up. . . .

Wish we had some real meat for supper. Piece of beef,
like. One more row and it'll be time. Cold beans. But sirup,
though. Wonder how Sister done at school today.

Down up. Down up. Down up. Jesus Christ, what a
cloud! Banked hard and black and throbbin while you
were in your choppin sleep. Don't no light rains come out
of the west. That sucker means business. Got his fists
drawed up to smash stuff. N where'd that gusty south
wind go? Crawled off somewhere an died. All puffed up
there in the west with blue-black mad. Says you know
what I'm gonna do. Gonna swell up and chunk hell out
of stuff with hailstones. Tellin you now with this here
jumpy air. Better high-tail it to the house, and never mind
gettin to the end of no row. Just tellin you, and you know
how much I'm a-jokin. Gonna sliver that young corn and
beat down that coat-button cotton.

"Nona!"

She looked up from her work after the third call. She
shook off hoeing and looked at him interrogatively.

"We better start for the house."

She glanced up at the sky and started across the field
as he had. The light was fading fast now, as the great
breathing cloud shut off the sunset glow. As they hurried,

a gust struck them out of the cloud. Then rain, instantly, coldly drenching, hurtled down on and over them. But they did not run until the hailstones began pelting them, beating their necks and shoulders, the forearms that were held over their eyes, as they ran, small and hurting, up the hill where Granny and Daisy waited, whooping, on the porch.

Then, pelted and dripping, they were inside building a fire. When they were dry, and the middling meat was frying, and the old house creaking before the driving wind, Sam closed his eyes and realized its great streaming force and knew he was under the sway of the enemy. Technically, of course, the storm was only Ruston's enemy. Actually it was Sam's too. And all men's. As were the weeds, and sickness. These were the things. You could not really feel the full implications of the storm without knowing that any conflict between men could never be more than internecine. And once you felt this, your patience grew shorter with the voices of hate. You came to know more clearly that whatever hand reached for the sword must be chopped off by the sword. Once you knew what Sam knew, that ignorance and disease, the blackness of the night and the terror of the storm, were the great eternal enemies of man, there could be no tolerance for those who sought to replace the processes of patient reason by violence, joint effort by war. More clearly could you see that whatever force sought to divide the people, on whatever pretext, was the enemy of the people, the toxin that would, if permitted, destroy their strength and blight their decent aspirations. Further, the storm told you that until humans could rise to the necessity to trust each other their vigor would be lost in disunion. It told you that if salvation, in the form of progress and fulfillment, were ever to come to men, it must come through intelligent trust, by rising above fear, and by means of the natural affection of man for man that automatically occurs when fear is removed, like the emergence of green leaves when winter is over.

In the other room, a wall board blew off and smashed against the floor.

"Father in heaven," Granny exclaimed, "don't let this here ole over-size privy blow down and squash us all!"

And Sam knew God wasn't listening, that He was too taken up with His storm.

Nona handed him his bread and bacon.

16

WHEN daylight came, Sam went out to survey the damage. All the corn was battered. Some of it in slivers. Much of the cotton was beaten against the earth, but the plants were so small that it had been hard for the hail to make many direct hits. Besides, they had possessed so much of the resilience of all young things that it was possible that even those which had been struck down would not die.

What happened next would be up to the crop itself. Sam went back in the house and ate breakfast.

This would have been a fine morning to bait out the fish lines except they were already most likely under water. However, the knowledge that the top of the ground would be alive with handy worms decided him to go have a look. And since he found the river up only a foot, most of the lines were accessible.

By eleven o'clock he'd caught a mess of small fish when Finley came stiff-legging it down to the river and said, "I'm goin in to town this afternoon. Want to go?"

It was entirely too wet to hoe cotton.

"Why not?" Sam said.

At twelve-thirty they started in, between the fields fat with rain, in Finley's old Chivvy, which he drove with the circumspection of a man whose reflexes are neither fast nor reliable.

"You haven't had no luck with ole Lead Pencil, have you?" he asked, driving.

"No," Sam said. "Had a couple of lines busted, though. What kind of luck has Henry had?"

"Bout the same as you."

"Thought you weren't goin to tell im."

Stickily Finley's gray eyes looked sidewise at Sam.

"Reckon I just forgot."

Before long they were passing the cemetery at the edge of Hackberry, then the cotton gin, and soon were among the thickening houses. The old car went on to Rat Row, a block of hamburger stands and beer joints where a fellow was likely to feel more at home than over on the other street where many of the people wore suits and neckties.

"Might as well go up to the domino hall," Fin said, "and see what's stirring."

Upstairs in the cool, dirty room, there were a dozen men watching one game.

"Who downed this here load of poles?" one of the players was asking.

"My pardner," another said. "If he was to down somethin he could up, it wouldn't be him."

"Hi, fellers," Sam said.

He knew most of them.

"There's my pardner," Johnny Kerr said. "Come on, Sam. Let's give em a lesson."

"Ain't got but one dime," Sam said, already realizing the delicious joy of his impending weakening, "and I meant to spend it on tobacco."

"Hell," Johnny said, squaring around to a table, "you can always mooch somethin to smoke. Sit down here."

"I ain't studied the backs of these rocks like you boys," Sam said. "Who wants to play us?"

A little man who was wearing a jumper instead of a shirt said, "Me and Aleck'll try to take on you experts. Come on, Aleck."

Sam liked Johnny Kerr. They used to fight each other as kids. Johnny was still pretty chesty and would fight anything that would make a track, but Sam liked him and remembered how when they played ball of a Sunday and Johnny was in the pitching box, you felt like you were getting somewhere.

"Stir em up, somebody," Sam said. When the dominoes were mixed, Sam took seven, in suppressed eagerness, anxious to join in this mathematical contest. He drew a hand of fives the first thing, downed the double, and said, "Gauge up ten for our side."

They played four games before Sam and Johnny lost one and Sam had to pay his dime.

"Come on," Johnny said. "Let's go down to Seaman's joint."

"To have a beer" was the tacit invitation, since it could not be voiced before so many.

"All right," Sam said.

"See you here later," Fin said forlornly.

In the beer joint there was nobody but big Seaman and an unappetizing tart named Lizzie, one of four or five who made Seaman's joint their headquarters.

"Hello, gents," Seaman said. "What'll it be?"

"Which kind of dime beer do you like best?" Johnny asked Sam.

"Whatever kind you get. I ain't had a beer since I can remember."

Johnny ordered, and Seaman set out the cold, wet, brown bottles.

"I guess I ain't supposed to get thirsty," Lizzie said.

"I wouldn't know," Johnny said. "If you do, take it up with your sweet papa there. He gets it wholesale."

She turned her back and filed on her fingernails.

Seaman set her out a bottle of beer.

"That ain't on me," Johnny said.

"No," Seaman said. "That ain't on you."

Johnny looked at his feet a minute and turned a little white around the mouth. He looked up at Seaman.

"Listen, Big Shot, I came in here to get a couple of beers—not to take any of your crap."

"You got em," Seaman said. "Drink em."

Johnny took a five-dollar bill out of his pocket.

"Gimme my change," he said. "You can take this God damned beer and shove it up your pratt."

Seaman took the money, rang up twenty cents, and gave Johnny eighty cents' change.

Johnny looked at it.

"All right," he said. "Give me that other four dollars, quick."

"What four dollars?" Seaman said, putting his hands under the bar. "Lizzie, you saw that was a one."

"Course I did."

"Give me that four dollars, you big double-jointed son of a bitch, before I tear this joint down."

Seaman's hand came out from under the bar holding a .45 revolver. Some of the nickel plating had curled off the cylinder.

"Outside," he said.

For a minute Johnny stood there.

"This ain't goin to do you no good," he said and went outside.

Sam followed him.

"What you goin to do?" Sam asked.

"I'm gonna get me a pile of rocks and get behind that yard-high curb an chunk hell out of him."

"Do," Sam said, "an he'll kill you."

Johnny got his rocks. Quarter-pound ones. About fifty.

They could see Seaman inside the joint talking to Lizzie.

From the curb Johnny took aim on Seaman's head and let fly. The rock missed by two inches, shattering half a dozen bottles. Seaman grabbed his gun and began shooting, and there was death and broken bones and mangled guts in every shot if Johnny didn't keep the heat on him with those rocks. Sam ran to the alley and began rolling more rocks to Johnny's feet. Then Sam hid behind a tree and tried to direct Johnny's aim, which was wild because Seaman was firing down on him and Johnny was having to keep half-way hid.

"Little lower there, boy," Sam called, "and to the right. Let's see this one smoke."

Sam had three rocks himself, but he kept watching out for the law and for a chance to throw. Then he saw Seaman cross over and start through a window in order to flank Johnny. Now once Seaman made it out that window, he could dash ten yards down the alley and have Johnny at point-blank range with nothing between them but air. And Seaman would burn Johnny down.

Sam slipped out from behind the tree, his fingers locked around a smooth rock, and cocked his arm. The whole focused attention of his being fixed itself on Seaman's head. He threw. And missed by inches. But the second one grazed the top of Seaman's head. It hit glancing or it would have knocked his brains out on the rocky alley.

"He's in the alley cold," Sam called softly to Johnny. "I reckon you'll have to take all the blame. I just didn't want to see you get shot. I'm on my way home."

"O.K.," Johnny said and started up the alley.

Sam slipped around an old warehouse to the domino hall and called Finley aside.

"Let's go," he said.

"What's the matter?" Fin said, coming alive at the smell of trouble.

"Nothin," Sam said. "Only I feel sick. I got to get home and lie down."

Ferdy Whiff caught them as the Chivvy started out of town.

"Come on down to the City Hall," he said.

Sam was scared. He knew Hackberry fighting justice. If you were standing on the corner and some stranger came along and knocked you down, you'd have to go to jail. Every fight was worth two fines to the justice of the peace and the constable. You could not get knocked down free of charge in Hackberry.

Ferdy had Johnny by the arm and Johnny was grinning.

"That son of a bitch really got his head skint," Johnny said. "I bet he don't try to short-change nair nother feller —for a week or so anyhow."

The justice of the peace was a tall old man with no teeth, waiting patiently, deafly, almost charitably, to assess the fines.

Seaman, his head tied up with a rag, made a sworn statement that it was a dollar bill and that Johnny, with Sam for moral support, had tried to highjack him.

Sam was thinking: "Ruston'll be sore. Crops don't wait while you lay out fines in jail."

Johnny told the truth like he was proud of it, like it was a good truth to tell. He referred to Lizzie—who was Seaman's star witness—only as The Virgin.

He knew he was going to have to lay out a fine, any-

way, and he might as well have some fun out of it. He
made everybody feel good, telling about it, except Seaman and The Virgin. He left Sam out of it completely.

Then Sam's time came and he said, "I'm glad to testify
as a pure spectator. But if you all are goin to play like I
was in it, I ain't puttin out nothin."

"The evidence will have to speak for itself," the justice
gummed, pleasantly, detached, "and you got to tell what
you know or you'll get fined for that too."

So Sam told how it started. How he'd tried to prevent
combat because he was afraid Johnny would be killed.

"But if Johnny was at the curb in front, how come
Seaman to get brained over by the window?" the justice
asked.

"Search me," Sam said. "I was so excited I didn't pay
no tention."

"You didn't assist Johnny with directions on how to
throw?"

"Well, if you seen a truck bout to run over a kid," Sam
said, "wouldn't you holler jump?"

"Maybe so," the justice said bleakly, feeling Sam was
eluding him, that there was no chance of a fine. "Won't
you even admit bein an accomplice after the fact?"

"No, sir. I never accompliced no part of this thing, and
I want to get home to my family. I got a little boy that's
sick."

"Well, then, go on," the old man said in despair, "and
next time keep plumb in or plumb out."

Sam left them adjudicating the damage to the beer joint,
which in the end had become a foaming shambles.

On the way out, he gave Johnny a warm, admiring smile. Johnny was a good man to do something with.

Outside, when he got in the car, Sam said, "Well, Fin, my sickness feels better now. Let's get on home."

And as they rode out of town Sam was full of the half-frightened exhilaration of escape from his brush with the law, feeling a warm, virile sense of comradeship with Johnny. And vividly remembering the fast, barely bent straightness of the throw that had peeled big Seaman's head, remembering the hot certainty he had felt while the rock was still in flight, while it was going nowhere on earth except to smack old Seaman on the head.

It had been a good day, and tonight he'd sleep with home wrapped snugly around him.

17

THE corn, which no longer showed any traces of damage from the hail, grew like plants in a myth. The cotton had left the coat-button stage and become soft, swelling spheres of dark green. But the corn, especially when you were accustomed to the wizened yield of the sandy land, was incredible, and you were rank with its growth and stunning virility. What magic stuff this black earth was! Even animals pastured on its grass far outgrew and outweighed those pastured in the sand hills, no matter how abundant the grass there might be.

And the rains ceased and the days grew hot, no longer warm but burning hot. From the house at noon you could see the shimmer of heat waves dancing over the fields, and

Granny carried a pasteboard fan, "Compliments of the Hackberry Burial Society," about the house with her and frequently remarked how nice a slice of cool watermelon would be.

Following the heavy rain and hail, the earth had first dried on top and baked into a shale that had to be crumbled with a plow. Then the sun drove and the thirsty roots pulled the moisture deeper into the ground so that cracks began to appear and to grow larger and deeper by the day.

One morning Sam found a baby quail which had fallen into one of these openings. The small bird was dead, caught there six inches below the surface in this crevasse, but it had not been abandoned without a struggle. Both sides of the crack had been pecked and scratched off by the other quail in an effort to rescue the victim, but the crack was too deep.

Because the cracks opened the nether earth to the parching rays of the sun, exposing roots, allowing the remaining moisture to escape, Sam plowed shallowly between the rows, powdering the surface so that the cracks were filled and covered.

None of Sam's immediate neighbors had crops as bold, as brave as his. Their land was the same, but he was getting more of himself into his crops, imparting more of the mule strength of Weaver and Frisno Emma to the cotton and the corn.

He could arrange things so that the life impulse in the corn might become drunk on growth. But for Jot, who lay in the hot bed the whole day through, he could do nothing. You could try. You could bring him milk when it was fresh and clean, before the flies got to it. He'd drink a little, but it did no good. He no longer had any taste for the delicacies from the garden, which the sun and dry weather were now so rapidly destroying. Sometimes he thought he'd like a piece of fried squirrel or chicken or even quail. You took time off and got it for him. Yet when you brought it, he'd turn away from it. Turn away the face that should have been all pink and white with smooth baby skin.

You felt his head. It was always hotter than your hand.

And you sat there, silent and helpless, feeling armless and legless against this enemy. You sat silently because if anybody said anything, the child began twitching and crying.

His suffering, his crying, his slow, visible disintegration into a corpse, were breaking your heart, beating your spirit into dust. But the doctor had said there was nothing to do.

One day Nona said, "There's a preacher holdin a meetin up the river they say can cure stuff."

"I don't know," Sam said. "There may not be nothin to it. Sometimes I've wondered if that ain't just for folks like us. Don't know nothin, ain't got nothin. For folks there ain't no cure for nohow. Just somethin to try, like."

"He's gettin awful bad, Sam. Ain't et since early yesterday."

Sam's face was blank with futility and despair.

"I'll tell you somethin," Nona said. "That night you stuck the cow, I prayed. I knew you didn't know what you were doin an I prayed."

"You figger that's what done it?"

"I don't know, Sam. But sometimes it seems like there's nelly got to be a Jesus. Things get so hard you can't stand em, an just keep on gettin worse." She knew somehow that that did not leave things quite right. It took something away from her husband's stature that should not be taken. "You been everthing to us, Sam," she said. "When it's groceries, when it's anything you can get your hands on, I don't fret. But you can't get no holt on this, can't get set to work against it. Maybe when it's like that, we got to have Jesus."

"I reckon," Sam said. "Looks like we ain't doin no good this way. An the baby's bout played out. I guess we better go."

Sam went out and sat on the edge of the porch.

"Jesus," he said quietly, "we done all we know how. Our baby's a-dyin. We're gonna hold im out to the preacher. Won't You please do what we can't do? Don't You think him and Nona's had bout enough?"

He walked across the yard, going nowhere except out of sight of the family. His face was wet and there was hope in his heart. He'd told Jesus so openly and honestly, with such purity of feeling and humility, that Jesus wouldn't turn him down. . . .

That night they went to the meeting and the preacher prayed over Jot, who wept miserably the whole time. Then he laid hands upon the child and pronounced him cured. Jot did not stop crying. They caught a ride home with some people in a truck.

The next day the child could eat nothing, but vomited at intervals, and when they touched his forehead, it was fiery hot.

"Take him back to the doctor," Nona said. "You got to."

Feeling abandoned by his God, that the baby would die on the road, Sam obeyed.

When Sam brought Jot into Dr. White's office, the doctor was sitting forward in his chair holding a stethoscope against a boy's chest. The doctor glanced at Jot and told the boy to leave and come back another time. In eccentric rhythms, rigors were shaking the child's wasted body.

"Bring him in here," the old doctor said.

Sam followed him into an adjoining room where there was an iron operating table with most of the white enamel chipped off.

A sparse clump of hair had fallen down on Dr. White's forehead. He was wonderfully dynamic now, hurrying cautiously. He nodded at the table and Sam put the baby on it. He dissolved a sedative tablet in water and injected the solution into the child's arm.

They both stood there watching Jot, and as the seconds became minutes, the rigors grew less sharply defined; the edge left his cries. In fifteen minutes he was asleep.

The old doctor shook his head nervously, his jaws and cheek bones and eyes full of a marvelous toughness that Sam involuntarily clung to.

"It's awful late to save that child," Dr. White said.

"Thank God," Sam thought, "he didn't say too late."

"Sit down," Dr. White said.

He lifted the baby onto the old brown tufted office couch.

"That baby's going to get some doctoring," the old man said. "They've got a new medicine called nicotinic acid. Drug store just got it in this week. It's supposed to cure what Jot's got. If it's not too late. . . ."

Sam sat there tense, silent, his nerves exhausted, looking at this old doctor who wanted to do something for Jot. It was enough to make you cry to feel how much he really wanted to help you when you were broke and he knew it.

For a moment longer Dr. White sat there looking in keyed-up blankness at the wall. Then he said, "I was a hunting man like you, Sam, a river man. I've always known everybody. The country people. The poor. The raggedy-assed. They were my folks. This same trouble Jot's got has carried lots of em away. I was supposed to stop it, but I didn't know how."

He was talking in the kind of tough trance that came natural to him.

"Your boy has been starving to death," he said. "By the time you could furnish him a good diet, he couldn't handle it. We'll feed him in his veins. I mean I will. And try the nicotinic acid. If it works, it'll mean more to me than when I killed my first deer. A hundred times more."

He picked up a nub of pencil off the desk and looked at it, talking.

"I'm getting old, I guess," he said. "But this is my town.

I came here fifty years ago. Time is like blood, Sam. It's
a whole lot thicker than water."

Then with a jerky movement he brushed his hair back
from his forehead. He went over to feel the baby's pulse.

The days that followed were the kind in which you
strive so hard to see every little telltale change that you
see many that aren't actually there. You watch the eyes,
hoping to see a positive thing come into them, hoping to
see there something besides the glaze of helplessness. Days
in which everything else stops. And you sit by a bed, in
a clear tense pool of hours, and watch the life impulse
in a small creature, its conscious will in abeyance, main-
tain its feeble struggle against the unknown, and against
the heat of the summer. And you know the crisis is here.
At no time has he ceased to get worse, and that is no longer
possible. What life remains is dim and vague and force-
less. Only a miracle will save the baby now, so you hope
for that, trying in every way to placate the gods. When
you start to the cow pen in the morning, it suddenly occurs to you that the gods might have a preference regard-
ing which path you take. You carefully wait for an ink-
ling of that wish and feel that you get it. You choose the
lower one. So it is when you go to take a match out of the
box. You feel you must look at all of them until one ap-
pears to be the one you should take. And if that match
doesn't strike the first time, it may seem to you a terrible
omen.

But for the past twenty-four hours has he actually got

any worse? Yesterday he was practically dead, and now, however weakly, he is still living. Another day passes, and the child's breathing, you almost dare to believe, is easier. But you know you are hoping so hard that what you think you are seeing is not to be trusted—unless it is bad news. Then you shake off waiting for a moment and realize a week has gone by. Maybe Jot actually is better.

And as the second week passes, a great compression of rejoicing, which you dare not yet express, begins to build inside you. But it has all happened so slowly it is hard to realize the improvement has been so great. It is now the fourteenth day of the new treatment, and Jot can bear sounds much better; he is beginning to have some semblance of an appetite.

Now, in comparison to that first one, the weeks are passing at a canter. In this third week Jot is wanting to be sung to, is calling for more food.

At last a whole month has elapsed since the first dose of nicotinic acid, and one day, while Granny is washing him in the dishpan, the baby stands on his tiptoes and out of sheer high spirits, out of the exciting joy of new health, wets forcefully, floodingly, in Granny's astonished face, then flies out of the house shrieking his accomplishment for all the world to hear.

And a lump comes in everybody's throat, even that of poor, drenched Granny, before this ecstatic triumph of life over death.

"I'm just so glad," the old woman says, standing there dripping, "that I'm a good mind not to wipe none of it off."

Before going outside to run down your naked, still happily shrieking child, you pause a moment at the door, realizing with profound relief that the days of terror are over.

18

SOON it would be time for the insects to assault the cotton. Not the leaf worms; they would come much later to denude the plants of foliage. But it was time for the boll weevils to come and sting the squares which later would become bolls. The stung bolls would never mature and open and hold out to you a fingered hand full of white cotton. They would die and rot. And in Sam's thinking, in his boll-weevil speculations, he thought how on wet years they were the worst, that moisture and shade were their friends, and the really murderous Texas sun their enemy.

Ruston would probably say poison, but poison and dampness would not be as good as poison and dry heat.

Beneath the leafy plant, where the sun never burned, the dew would linger and the bugs would thrive. There on the ground no poison would fall. Just under the plant would be their sanctuary. Now he would destroy even that last retreat. Conscript gravity and the sun against them.

He hitched his team and began plowing the fine crumbles of earth into a high ridge whose peak ran down the line of stalks, leaving no plateau of earth in the stalks' own shade, but only a steep plane, so that the larvae, falling from the plant itself, would tumble into the unshaded furrow, there to be killed by the sun.

It was on the fourth day of this job that he saw Ruston's car stop down at the road, saw him go for a careful walk over the lower field and then come into the upper one.

"Why, Sam," he said, apparently surprised, "I can't see where you've ruined any cotton with that sweep."

"Was I sposed to?"

"How are the mules making it?"

"All right. They'll keep on makin it."

"Everything going along smooth?"

"Well, I'd kinda thought so. . . . Mr. Ruston, what the hell did you mean, I don't seem to have plowed up no cotton?"

"Nothing. I just heard you was shaving em pretty close."

"That's to roll the bugs out into the sun."

"I know."

"Well, are you satisfied with how I'm doin?"

"Yes. You've got a good crop. I got to run on now. Just passing. See you later."

His knees bending a little too far back, he went to his car and drove off.

"Get up, mules," Sam said.

The only way Ruston or anybody else could hear a thing was for somebody to tell him. In this case, it had been such a bold lie that it could only have been told out of malice. So somebody was gunning for him. And though there were no concrete reasons for suspecting anyone, there seemed every probable reason for feeling it must have been Henry. That was just the sort of thing he'd do. But why? To raise himself in his own and Ruston's opinion by depreciating his neighbor? Or was he coveting the sixty-eight acres which he would be in a position to work with his own equipment? There was no telling. But Sam was worried.

The summer days began almost in the middle of the night, it seemed, and ended there. To Granny they were not unpleasant. There was generally a breeze on the hill and she was monarch of the house while Sam and Nona were away all day in the field. Her will was Jot's law and Zoonie's. Daisy, the insurrectionist, much to Granny's satisfaction, spent most of the time tagging after her parents or visiting over the neighborhood. And throughout the long days, Granny happily fulfilled her office of Commander-in-Chief, pro tem, of the Premises.

To Granny, all time was the present and, except for such crises as when Jot would grab the butcher knife and start running from her, or when she'd set down one of her afternoon snacks and Zoonie would steal it, the present was under control. Actually the past had dissolved. It was too big and dim and remote. And, of course, at seventy-three there are more reassuring pursuits than dwelling too strongly upon the future.

Everything was just the summery present, with no rheumatism to speak of, and a baby and a dog to play with. Little things to play with and instruct, to harangue into your own image. And your decisions and edicts were made and delivered with full confidence. You knew Jot and Zoonie did not know better than you. So you stuck to your guns and made what you said stand up.

Or if one of your useful moods came on you, you went out into the garden and picked some of what the sun had left, and boiled it for dinner. Only, if it was potatoes, they looked pretty bad by the time you got them cooked, because you had punched them so much with a fork wanting to see if they were done—in reality, trying to prod them into getting done faster. You knew when you were doing it you were spoiling them, crumbling them to mush, but you were curious and tired of waiting and kept on punching them every little while. And when you finally took them off the stove and they seemed to have been shot with a shotgun at close range, you were discouraged and thought, "I don't never have no luck with nothin." But if you forgot them and let them burn up, you just buried them and didn't say anything. You were too old to bother yourself with any such trifles as that.

That Daisy, now. She was something else again. Little

Tartar. Just as soon sass hell out of you as look at you, and if she got mad enough, liable to pick up a stick and go for you. Scuse you, from havin no such child as that. Smart though, Sam said. Real smart. Only she really needed her butt wore off about twicet a day. Except Sammy boy was in the field and Nona . . . that Nona. However in the world come him to pick such a outfit as that? Just go around sullin at a person. Don't never make over you the least little bit about nothin. Mean's what she is. N ignorant, you reckon. Don't know ole folks sposed to be treated with respect.

Then the nice girl that Sam should have married begins talking to you. She is not anybody you ever actually met or heard of, but is very real to you because she is one of the friends and admirers that exist in your imagination. She is the anti-Nona that brings comfort when ole Nona gets after you. "Pore Granny dear," this sweet, imaginary granddaughter-in-law says, "what can I bring you nice to eat? You're so old an wonderful an seen so much, such a joy to have around. Cook up all that good stuff while we're in the field an watch after Jot so good an Zoonie and mean Daisy. Maybe you'd like for me to tan her tail, Granny dear, just on general principles? Just cause me an you know she needs it."

So sweety nice nice, and not like that ole mean Nona. Some folks don't know how lucky they are. She's got all this wonderful family, an Sam ain't off diddlin all the time like other men an . . . "Put that saucer down, Jotty boy. . . . Cause I said so, that's why. . . . Are you or ain't you? . . . Oh! You say you ain't!"

And the mesquite switch is on the mantel, the one ole sullen beat you up with, and you grab it and begin switching Jot's legs and that plague-taked Zoonie rears up and takes a high, meat-catchin bite in the back of your skirt and swings on like a snappin turtle.

Then when Daisy comes in, she finds you and Jot both blubberin, and you tell her how Jot and the dog have insulted you.

And the little hellion laughs.

All the while, daily, hourly, the corn had been growing fast. In two weeks' time, say by the Fourth of July, topping could begin. Already the ears were full length, and only the kernels themselves were as yet immature. The tassels, each like a sparse handful of askew straws, had issued from the top of the stalks. The silks had long since lost their bright neutrality of color and were red and brown and every color between, including some with an admixture of deep purple.

"We need a good rain now while the corn's in silk an tossel," Sam said.

And a heavy, soaking rain came.

For a couple of days, then, farm work had to be suspended. On the morning after the rain Sam had taken his single-shot .22 and gone to the woods, easing along the bottoms, pausing now to sit beneath a bush, again to lean against a tree, watching for the brisk movements, listening for the small sharp crackling sounds that squirrels make early in the morning. He had already killed two, which would make a meal for his family, but he was eager to get a couple for old man Hewitt.

This morning he had made Zoonie stay at the house, because the character of the bottom woods would have made him more a liability than an asset. The bottom timber was too large either to climb or to cut except in special instances. The only way to hunt it was with stealth, to leave boldness to the squirrels. For unlike the situation in the post oaks, where your object was to drive them into a hollow and then chop them out, any squirrel that went into the hollow of one of these great trees would be safe, for the reason that the job of getting him out was considerably greater than his worth to the hunter. Here squirrels must be seen and shot as they traveled abroad.

But while Sam was sitting on a rotten log, scanning the treetops, alertly listening, his attention was attracted by large numbers of bees flying around the little patches of wild flowers: horse mint and sunflowers, the snow-white blossoms of thistles, which grew wherever the sunlight could reach the forest floor.

Now the presence of so many bees could mean but one thing, that somewhere, perhaps at a considerable distance, there was a bee tree. And in that bee tree there would not only be honey, but, if the hollow was big enough, a great deal of it.

The abundant rains earlier in the year had lighted the whole countryside with Indian blanket, wild violets, buttercups, and bluebonnets by the thousands of acres. Every fruit tree and flowering bush had bloomed wonderfully. As a honey year, this one had been above the average.

Eager to trace their route to the tree, Sam fixed his whole attention on the winding flight of the bees, but none of them seemed to be either going to or coming from any special place.

"Buggers is just on the prowl. Ain't many flowers in these ole shady woods. Have to keep on lookin, tryin to get em up a load fore goin home. But, by jookies, the ones that goes for water's bound to get enough o that at one place. Ones that's packin it home, bound to go straight there from the river."

Being careful to keep in the general range of activity of the bees, Sam went over to the river. Here where the water stood still and shallow and welled up around but not over the pieces of gravel at its edge, the bees were taking water. Many of them actually seemed to be drinking out of the small, unimmersed tops of little porous stones, up through which Sam supposed the water rose like kerosene up a lamp wick.

To this watering place the bees were coming from random directions, but once they had taken water they all flew away in the same direction and their route was straight.

Sam smiled and waded the river. As a boy he'd helped adults rob bee trees, had carried buckets and helped chop, but he'd never handled the bees himself. Even so, he knew that the first rule was to be gentle with the bees and unafraid. He could not afford to ask some bee man for help because that would cost him half the honey. He must do it himself, relying on care and horse sense to see him through.

As he climbed out on the other bank, he could see the bees flying higher and higher, but in the clear sunlight they were still visible, and the straightness of their flight made it easy to follow.

Walking on, he was hoping hard that no one had found and marked the tree already. If it had been previously located and not yet robbed, it would be marked with an X, and that mark would have to be respected. An X on a bee tree meant as much as a brand on a cow. A man who robbed a marked tree was not an opportunist. He was a thief.

Sam had gone some two hundred yards from the river when he reached his destination, when he saw the bees there above him passing into the hollow of a tall dead elm. And a kind of golden excitement possessed him, an excitement that comprised something of the quality of fantasy. The whole idea of taking quantities of honey straight from the hand of nature had an appeal for Sam that was nameless because it was poetic.

For a moment he stood watching the brisk, orderly ingress and egress of bees from the tree hollow. Then, almost feverishly, he began examining the tree for marks. When, to his great relief, he found none, he cut a cross on the barkless trunk. On second thought he added in small, shallow letters beneath it: *S. Tucker*.

Now as he hurried home for the necessary implements, his whole mind was in a turmoil of planning how he would go about robbing the tree, which way he'd want it to fall, how he'd apply the smoke, what kind of container he'd need for the honey, how much help he'd require.

Nona would have to assist him. The kids would be a nuisance and might get stung.

At the house he told Nona the news in private. And on her face too Sam could see the oblique pleasure that is more exquisite because something of the unexpected, the extraordinary and exotic, is involved.

"We'll need the tub and that nail keg the tub sets on," Sam said. "And the ax and a piece o tow-sack with no holes in it an some rags and a piece o wire."

When these things had been collected, and Sam and Nona were on their way to the bottoms, she said, "What's the nail keg for?"

"Maybe you'll laugh," Sam said, "but after we get the honey out into the tub, I mean to try to catch the bees an put em in the keg."

"To raise?"

"We ain't fixed for that. But I figgered some o the regular bee folks'd pay money for a keg o wild bees. All they got to do is set em in a hive an let em make honey. Like as not, folks'd want em to liven up their own strain."

"How you gonna get em in the keg?"

"Just put em in, I reckon. One time somethin happened that give me a clue. Havin a funeral down in the country, and bout the time they commenced carryin the box out the house, these folkses' bees swarmed. Natchully that was a disturbance to the funeral and the widow lady just says, 'Wait a minute,' an went in the house an come out with a dishpan an commenced beatin on it. Says, 'That'll settle them scogies,' and by God it did. They balled up on a fence post and stayed put till the funeral got away."

"Aw," Nona said.

"So I figgered if these swarmed, I'd beat the tub and when they balled up, just slip the keg over em and rake em off; then put that piece of tow-sack over the top."

Nona smiled.

"You sure got some ideas, ain't you?"

"Well, if it don't work, it just don't work. Don't cost nothin to try."

When they reached the tree, Sam cut a long green branch, trimmed it, and wired the wad of rags on the end.

"This here is our smoker," he said, "in case we need to smoke out the bees. Now I'll cut down the tree. Them bees get after us, I spec we better run jump in the river."

"Maybe they won't," Nona said. "Cut it down."

And Sam began driving the blade into the base of the tree. Twenty minutes later the elm leaned and crashed to the ground, its great, dry limbs snapping like kindling, the limb which grew outside the hollow being wrenched off in such a way that a panel was torn the full length of the five-foot hollow.

The sight before them in the opened hollow was stupendous. In the lower portion of the comb were the larvae. In the upper was what must be some forty pounds of honey. And above that, around the inside of the hollow, was the crawling mass of tough, armed insects, many layers thick. Yet while the tree fell, and even afterward, only a very few of the bees made any effort to fly outside.

"Bring the tub," Sam said. "They're stunned."

With a piece of split-off wood he began scooping out the amber, translucent comb.

When the honey was in the tub, Sam said, "Bring the keg."

Already bees were beginning to cover his arms, his upper body.

Obeying, Nona said, "They ain't in no ball. You can't get em."

"There's a little ball here on one side. I'm gonna take it out and set it in the keg. When I do, cover it up. Then we'll beat the tub and the others'll ball up somewhere."

Carefully, gently, he placed his hand beneath the apple-sized ball of bees, lifted it out, and set it in the keg. Quickly Nona covered it with the burlap and held the cover on. Then while Sam was looking around for a stick with which to beat the tub, she called, "Sam! They're comin after me."

He turned and saw the bees whirling about her.

"Back away!" he yelled. "Back steady! Don't beat at em!"

Then, strangely, almost miraculously it seemed to them, as Nona backed away, futilely holding the keg cover out in front of her, the bees did not follow her. Instead, first the ones that had swarmed around her, then the others in the hollow, did the one thing neither Sam nor Nona expected.

All of them, the whole hive, flew into the keg and settled there.

When they were all inside, Sam said, "Well, Jesus Christ!"

He took the cover from Nona and fixed it on the keg.

"I guess the queen musta been in that first little hand-ful," he said. "Knowed the rest'd foller her but I hadn't no idea where she was."

Now, with Sam carrying the honey, and Nona the bees, they started home.

After giving the Hewitts five pounds of honey, Sam sold ten in town for six cents a pound. An old man with a glass eye gave him seventy-five cents for the bees. But Sam had brought another five pounds in two quart fruit jars. These he left on Dr. White's back steps without knocking or leaving any note.

As he hurried away down the alley, his satisfaction over the whole honey episode was rich and full. And he was particularly delighted to have been able to give his friends presents of this woods-found delicacy, the very wildness and secret derivation of which placed it outside the realm of things which can be valued in money. To Dr. White it would be even better because he'd never know where it came from.

Walking on down the grassy alley, Sam simply had to have someone to talk to, someone to whom he could tell intimate things with some assurance of being understood.

"God," he said, as he sidestepped a piece of jagged blue glass in an old ash heap, "there's some nice things happens to a man. Not only that. There's some pretty things. Real pretty and . . ."

The images, the message, fused into the exquisitely in-expressible. A kind of delicious embarrassment possessed him which he turned off into a happy humming of an old song:

> *Rye whisky, rye whisky,*
> *Rye whisky, I cry.*
> *Rye whisky, rye whisky,*
> *I'll drink till I die.*

As he walked on up the alley, he saw the magnificently large and protuberant buttocks of a Negro woman bending over a washtub, saw a bony, brown dog digging a curled meat rind out of a garbage bucket, saw three green bottles on a kitchen porch flashing in the sun, saw a red-headed woman in a back yard drying her hair against a brilliant white towel. And it seemed to him he'd never seen such a series of surgingly pretty sights in all his time.

By early July the corn crop was mature. There was a magnificent heft of stalk, and a firm, cutting toughness of the ridged blades. Its color was almost sinister. Had you wanted to paint a wagon to match it, and had your paint been the pale green of sand corn, you'd have had to add great quantities of midnight blue. Somehow its color suggested to you all the drunken, creative surge that you felt to be in this growth-charged land.

Nor was the corn merely fine to look at; the full ears were there, two and three to a stalk. And Sam began slashing off the corn tops with a home-made machete, bundling them, studding the fields with shocks of fine fodder.

Yet as he worked, a soft, encompassing sadness began

to possess him because none of that fodder would accrue to him, and he felt a strange inclination almost to weep when the wagons came and hauled it off.

It wasn't his. He'd made a trade and, he told himself, he didn't make any little-boy trades.

Or had he only gone through the motions of making a trade? Hadn't he just promised to pretend this fodder wasn't his?

He didn't want it to sell. He just wanted it. It was a part of him, a thing made partly of his own will and sweat and secret decisions.

He felt awful, but they took it off and he did not let anybody know how he felt. He had promised to pretend it wasn't his.

Then a Negro came by one day and told Sam something he'd heard on the commissary porch.

"We uz all jess settin there," the Negro said, "and this here feller say, 'I certainly wisht I had it easy like ole Sam Tucker. Jess fiddle around the creek all night, fishin for ole Lead Pencil, an drowsin round the fields all day thout no overseer there to make me put out.' "

"That son of a bitch said that to Ruston?" Sam asked.

"Yes, sir. Don't get me messed up in this thing, Mr. Sam. I'd be plumb ruint. But I knowed you so long an all, I jess hated for you to get run down to the Boss Man like that thout you knowin it. How come, you reckon, he done that?"

"I guess cause this place is makin a better crop than his. All he's got to do is look out the window to see it," Sam said. "Probably wants to rent it out from under me."

An hour later Sam saw Henry going to the mail box and went to intercept him.

"Hello," Henry said.

"What have I ever done wrong to you, Henry?"

"Why, nothin, Sam."

"Henry, you been talkin too much with your mouth."

"How's that?"

"To Ruston."

Henry's right hand slipped into his pocket where his knife was.

"I joke a heap with ole Ruston," he said.

"A man's a God damned fool to start trouble with his neighbors," Sam said. "Trouble is a bad thing. If I was you, I wouldn't joke no more about me ruinin cotton with a plow or not puttin in good days from sun to sun."

Sam's square jaw was set. His eyes flashed with anger.

Henry did not attempt a denial.

"Well," he said, "I won't."

Sam turned and left.

19

SUNDAYS were good, really substantially good, and if you were a river man, never lonely or dull. They began when you opened your eyes at dawn with the weight of another day's work hanging over you. Then you realized it was Sunday, and that long, depleting responsibility, which on less lucky days only a day of drudgery could satisfy, simply vanished, just because it was Sunday, and your body lay there grateful in the bed. But the deliciousness of the bed soon began to fade. This was Sunday, inviting and adventurous. The creek was just down the hill.

Later you were going to be extra hungry because all your stomach had to do was rest up and dream about dinnertime, knowing dinner today would not be built around fried salt jowl but some unpredictable thing that you'd devote the morning to catching. By noon or one o'clock there would most certainly be a turtle soup or a gar stew or a fried fish, perhaps a rabbit with dumplings, or a squirrel. You could never tell, and that was what made it piquant and exciting.

"I see you over there bein awake," Daisy would say, or Granny would want to know if anybody had any idea of building a breakfast fire tween now and Christmas. Then Jot and Zoonie, full of morning, would be scrambling spiritedly on the floor, and the family would be awake and all delighted with the fact that it was Sunday.

After breakfast the whole family, except Granny, would go as far as the swimming hole together, where Nona and Daisy would hold one end of the minnow seine while Sam pulled the other end over the gently sloping edge of the pool or down the shallow, gravel-floored rapids below it. A good catch of minnows would set the children wild and they'd help gather the little silver flipping fish quickly with carefully wetted fingers, and put them in the bucket. Sometimes a water moccasin would get caught in the seine and there would be tremendous excitement and big-eyed dancing and shrieking. Or if there were grasshoppers about and the river was clear, there would be a hopper hunt and this, too, would not be without a good deal of laughing and shrieking, and exhibitions of prize specimens and discussions of tactics. Or perhaps Sam would choose to dig for bait and let the children pick the enormous, dangling worms out of the broken clods, or the clean, white sawyers out of the split wood, in case he'd brought the ax. Again, with nice thrusts of forefinger and thumb they would gather hellgrammites from the gravel. Though if he planned to use the larvae of wasps, he'd wait until the others were gone before knocking down a nest.

When there was bait aplenty, Sam would begin the arduous task of getting away without the children. Under ordinary circumstances he could manage it and Nona would keep them there at the swimming hole and wash them and herself in the river, afterward taking them to the house. But if there were lines to run in the boat, it was not always possible to get off without Daisy. Besides, she could swim like a swamp rabbit and, when Jot wasn't there, would keep reasonably still. However, if a special line had been set the night before for Lead Pencil, the family would go with Sam to look at that one. He thought it would be educational for them to see such a sight if old Lead was on the line.

When fishing for Lead, Sam usually plaited three regular lines together, put a big hook on the end of it, and baited with a half-pound fish. Sometimes when they went to these special lines on Sunday morning, the bait fish was still there, swimming desperately in red-eyed exhaustion. Other times the bait was gone and there would be no telling what had got it—gars perhaps, or turtles. Now and then the line would be broken. Once, one of the big hooks was straightened. And once again the line looked pretty definitely cut. But whether or not it had been, remained a mystery.

In any case, Sam had engaged the monster, had found

a place where he fed. One of these days perhaps . . .

Then when the others were gone, Sam would begin
reading the stream for this day's fishing, building a set of
probabilities in his mind and acting on them. Or if he
were fishing for buffalo, he'd simply put a wad of stiff
dough on the point of his hook, shove the stubby pole into
the bank, and wait, enjoying this pleasant bodily communion with the earth, or perhaps losing himself in the life
there before him, half seen, half felt, in the river.

On one of these Sundays Sam found that the little
woolly worms were falling from the trees into the water,
little worms that were a soft cloudy green, all whiskery
with high, stiff, white hairs, striped transversely with
bright henna markings. They were tumbling ten a minute
onto the water of the moving channel, and beginning to
inch their way, high and dry, on the surface across the
stream to a drift of wooden debris. All of them without
exception were taking this long route across the stream
to the same place, inching along unmolested, while from
the river's floor the bass of the stream and the channel
catfish quietly watched their progress, themselves moving
patiently with this procession until it neared the drift.
Within the catacombs of the drift, the perch too were
watching, trying to calculate the exact instant to dart
out from the drift, just ahead of and faster than the rest
of their waiting kind, and yet not daring to venture so far
that the larger fish could catch them before dashing back
to safety. Sam knew that the streaking drama would occur
at the edge of the drift when the larger creature attacked
the smaller as it, in turn, came out to attack the still

smaller. And fast, explosively, it happened: the tiny ring of water when a perch, with a small, quick, sucking sound, sucked in a worm, and then the big electric boil as a larger fish, driving in a fast arc to the surface, nailed the perch and returned to its observation point below.

Quietly Sam went downstream. A less careful observer would have supposed the big fish had struck at the green worm, not having noticed the tiny ring into which the worm had disappeared half a second earlier. Crossing at the next shallow place, he came back upstream, took a three-inch perch out of his bait bucket, and put it on his hook. He then maneuvered it in short sorties from the drift in the direction of the approaching worms. Soon afterward, he had a two-pound channel cat. Within the next hour he caught a three-pounder and a two-and-a-half-pound bass.

It had been a wonderful morning, filled with drama, with sharp analysis and understanding. He took his fish home, feeling like a lord of the earth, an alert Indian, a man who had devised a good way to meet the peculiar exigencies of that morning.

Lead Pencil had not entered into that morning at all, even as a consideration. For Lead Pencil was old, probably older than Sam, and his ways would be definite. He was a good fish with all the protective instincts of his kind brought to a state of high development. Beyond question, whatever old Lead ate, he would eat nocturnally. The light of day would be hateful to him. Like babies and puppies and all young things, the little catfish must feed frequently, be it day or night. But old Lead would kill big fish only on moonless nights and go to a cave and digest them for a week, more likely ten days. You could get the blacksmith to make a great hook out of the brake rod of an old car, and it would hold any fish, but would Lead take it? There needed to be a little more thinking done.

Then on Sunday afternoons a few of the fellows sometimes gathered by the river and played penny-ante poker. Perhaps there'd be two or three Negroes from up the river and maybe a Mexican or two from a big farm down the road, and clappy Fin and a few of the other white boys of the neighborhood. Fifteen or twenty cents would get you in the game. And table stakes were the rule. Or maybe if you were broke but were known to be a careful, cagey player, and one of the fellows had no partner, he'd stake you and give you a quarter-portion of what you won. For it was openly understood that you needed a partner in this game in order to keep the other players' good hands in the middle, for tactical maneuvers of raising and re-raising. That was the way Sam usually played. And Sam would play anybody's money like it was his own, turning the bad hands over.

Once one of the Jackson boys introduced a deck of marked cards into the game, but none of the other players said anything until they had won all his money on the windies he tried to run. Then they laughed at him. They had all been brought up on marked cards and doctored dice and had known exactly what cards he held while he was betting on the assumption that they didn't.

But sometimes Sam began Sunday on late Saturday afternoon. That is, he would go to the river then, having got one of his neighbors to take his grocery list and the money into town. Once Nona even went into town in a neighbor's car, leaving Sam free to go to the river. And when you begin in late afternoon when it's quiet in the bottoms and your lines are baited and there's just you and a boat and a smoky lantern, it is not the same place at all that it is on Sunday morning. On Sunday morning it is sunshiny with clarity; everything is obvious and you can see what the creatures of the river are doing. It is fine and sparkling, but it is not night on the river, which comes earlier than up on the fields.

Then, slowly, as the night matures, the big fish slide out from the banks. The south wind moans through the trees. The water moccasins glide into the weeds or up into the overhanging willows and look down your neck as you float underneath them in the boat. And the eyes of the water tarantulas reflecting the lantern light are bright red-and-blue little rings, and the skunks are a-prowl, and the coons. This is their time and their place and you have violated it. They are looking at you in the dark and smelling you and hearing you. Just outside the small dim circle of lantern light they are watching you, and all you see is the flame of the lantern.

On the river at night you are not an individual, but a human that is there, and the time is no longer a particular century. Time, as a thing of transience and flux, is no longer applicable. It exists with validity for you only as a vast continuum whose beginning and end are alike and whose course has been without essential change.

You smoke. About you things rattle the bushes and you

don't know what they are. A fox may come up and look at you in mild astonishment, and go daintily on his way. A screech owl rubs your nerves with his emery voice.

If you were ever to see the gods, say, see them come walking down a leaning tree, wearing shiny orange robes, this would be the place. Here the extraordinary thing is not necessarily the unexpected one. At any time the river may starkly abandon its old channel and leave a dry ditch where it had been comfortable for a few centuries. And the willows and the frogs, whose lives are bound to it, will follow it to its new course. Once this little river rose in the night and drowned ninety people, left mules and bales of cotton caught in the tops of the highest trees. And yet it is as certain as it is erratic. It was flowing before you came, when you were just nothing, and will still be flowing after you are gone. Its creatures will go on devouring each other. When every tree in the bottom has lived out its life, there will still be the river, and another fellow will come down and sit by it, and his wife will wash her babies in the river. Will somebody take away that fellow's fodder?

Sam had no way to answer that, but there was something else he'd been trying to get his hands on: just how he felt about Ruston's trucks hauling off the fodder he himself had raised. Was owning the main thing, the meaningful thing? Or making? Making fine stands of fat fodder where there wasn't anything before?

"Maybe I ain't got much sense, studyin about such as that," he thought. "I guess that's boy stuff."

But he wanted to know, and he kept running his fingers over how he had felt, and began to be astonished by the conviction that the making was the main thing, that a man could feed off the making. You somehow had the feeling, when with simple, laborious magic you were making good things out of dirt and time and weather, that you were paying your dues in that big association known as the human race.

And there, alone in the river-night thinking, he began to understand the reason for a lot of satisfaction and contentment he had felt in times past, satisfactions that he had candidly attributed to his own ignorance and a sort of ingrained sense of peasanthood that he presumed he should be ashamed of.

Now he believed he saw a sensible reason for it.

On one of Sam's rare and brief departures from the land, he had worked in the Ford factory in Houston and earned five dollars a day. He was single then, and that was in boom times. He had never dreamed of making so much money in his life. Every time a car came by on the conveyor, he attacked the front fender and door with a ball of rags smeared with a compound to cut the paint down to the bottom of the pores that had formed in it during the baking process. He'd had to work at top speed every minute, pressing hard on the rag ball, taking long-range, careful strokes, the while walking with the passing car. It couldn't wait for you to finish, you had to work on it on the fly. And somehow it all made you angry, because a brisk pace was not fast enough, because you had to make a continuous, high, straining effort four hours at a stretch.

Five dollars a day. Each car smelled like hot banana oil. You worked furiously and earned five dollars a day.

After two weeks he quit.

"What's the matter?" the foreman asked. "You looked like you were doing all right."

"I don't know," Sam said. "It just don't seem to do me no good."

"Five bucks a day!" the man said.

"Mister," Sam said, "I ain't really smart. But you could give me this God damned factory and I wouldn't rub no more fenders. Can't you see I hate the son of a bitch? It's eatin me up."

The thing was that a man could not have the proper diet rubbing fenders. It took all that stuff out of you and didn't put anything back. When it used up what you had had to start with, you were empty and finished.

"What about them pore bastards that do it year in an year out?" Sam thought. "What do they get out of it?"

But no matter how many times he asked himself this question during the nights alone beside the river, the answer was always the same, anemic and insufficient: five dollars a day.

Then with almost a feeling of shame for the richness of his own way of life, when so many thousands of other men must undergo the steady desiccation of the spirit that factories impose upon them, he would flip his cigarette into the weeds and walk down to the red boat, get into it, and start smoothly up the river, most of the time simply guiding the boat, shifting from eddy to eddy, up the dark stream to a willow limb that by now would be thrashing the water.

20

LITTLE squares come first, the shape of a tiny snap purse, and if these escape being stung, they open into white flowers that a day or so later turn pink. Then the flowers are gone and in their place a boll is forming. When it is the size of your thumb, it is hard as a green plum. Its inside is glossy white and the fibers are not yet separate things.

If a great drought has been on, the bolls fall off on the ground and rot. But only if there has been a truly great one. For when the burning, scalding sun is bending the weeds down to the earth, and the near-by row of feed is turning brown, is slowly, literally, giving up the ghost for lack of water, then the cotton is just falling into its

stanchest, most comfortable rhythm, is being given a
chance to use its great powers. It is prepared, and likes
for the sun to do its worst. All the cotton that sun would
kill has died seedless long in the past, and this cotton, Sam's
cotton, has made arrangements in advance against dry
weather. It has sent, boring down to spectacular depths,
a tap root which is to have a rendezvous with moisture
when none is left near the surface of the earth, when men
are mulching topsoil with a plow to fill the plummeting
cracks that are opening in the earth.

Ruston said to poison. He was one of those big cotton
fellows and could say it. He had the money to buy the
poison, and sent a contraption that would blow it on the
cotton. There had been more rain than was actually
needed. The weather had been on the bugs' side. So Sam
hitched up and began poisoning.

On clear mornings you were shooting the deadly dust
on the cotton when daylight came, having got ready in
the night. You were fogging it onto the dark green leaves,
and the dew was making it stick. Every five days you
poisoned the whole works. Ruston said that was the scien-
tific way. Said it cost like hell, and an overflow might
still come and wash the crop away, but he just wasn't
raising cotton for no God damned bugs to have a picnic
on. Sam liked that and put the poison to the cotton.

And when the leaf worms began to sweep over the
country and the night air was sickeningly sweet with the
smell of their work, when the cotton of Sam's neighbors
was beginning to grow naked and there was nothing left
of the leaves but the skeletons, Sam's cotton was not

harmed. The bugs came to the edge of his fields, but that was as far as they got. The bottom cotton was standing breast-high and was loaded with bolls, twenty, thirty, sometimes forty to a stalk. You could look at it and tell that none of the elements that went into its making was feeble or indifferent.

One day at noon as Sam was coming out of the lower field, he met old man Hewitt, who was on his way down to the bottoms to soak and swell his wagon wheels in the river.

"Whoa," the old man said to his mules, setting them back on their haunches with the lines.

"Kinda summertime, ain't it?" Sam said, dripping with sweat.

"Kinda," the old man said. "What's the news?"

"Don't know it, only I been wantin to tell you that goofy calf has pretty well got onto hisself."

"Glad to hear it. Seen im the other day and he peared to have a right smart of vinegar for him."

"What I been wonderin," Sam said, "is about Uncle Walter. That's what the kids call the cow. She comes in heat, but it don't do her no good. If you want her to throw a calf next spring, we're gonna have to beat what we're a-doin."

"I ain't got anything to breed er to," the old man said thoughtfully, "sidesin maybe a dominicker rooster. Reckon you could look around and scare up somethin?"

"Like as not. What kind of calf did you have in mind?"

"I don't know, Sam. If she does any worse'n last time, I don't hardly dare think how it'll be."

"I mean, do you want it for milk stock or beef?"

"It don't matter much. She's not likely to have anything very fancy, no matter what you breed er to. Whatever you can find, long as it's free."

"All right, sir," Sam said. "I'll tend to it."

The old man drove on to the river.

Walking home Sam gave his entire attention to the problem of breeding the cow. To him it was a far less trivial matter than to the old man. Uncle Walter was a trust. Sam meant to return her in the fall not only with a healthy yearling at her heels, but with a calf inside her, and one with the maximum possibilities, considering Uncle Walter's nondescript nature and his own inability to hire the services of a good bull. To breed her to just any old scrub would be a shoddy thing and a non-joyous one. It would rob the future of any very hopeful speculation concerning the calf. But if a good bull could be obtained, one that would start the embryo on its life-path with promise and virility, that would be a fine and rewarding thing. There was always something about a good bull that set you dreaming. You felt a warmth for him because he was a giver, a creator, because you knew he would infuse his own dynamic, forever regenerative strength into hundreds of calves.

By the time he got home, Sam was, actually, almost afire with an idea. He called Nona outside to discuss it with her.

"The old man wants the cow bred," Sam told her, "and he asked me to tend to it. Listen, Nona, you know that bunch of prize Herefords across the river?"

She nodded. Like Sam and a good many others, she had taken the trouble to go look at them, to drink in the stanch, moving beauty of a hundred square, fat Herefords with their quiet, box-shaped calves, each cow wearing her registration number on her horn. There were three fine bulls in separate pens, but one of them, called The Red Duke, was the grand champion of the Hackberry stock show and three other county shows. His owner, Harley Murphy, who had the gin a few miles up the road, had refused three thousand dollars for him, and would not, of course, allow this bull to be bred to the likes of Uncle Walter at any price.

"What I mean to do," Sam said, "is sneak her across the river some night and let The Red Duke have a go at er."

"Maybe you better not," Nona said. "Somethin might happen. You get caught, you might get put in jail."

"I don't aim to get caught," Sam said. "Sides, think how proud the old man'd be when I told im after it was all over."

"You know best," she said, "but it sounds risky to me."

"I'm gonna try it," he said. "I may get et up alive if they find me there. But the old man's been so good to us, seems like we owe him a risk or two. She'll come in heat again this week. And this time it won't go to waste."

All that week Sam kept a careful watch on the cow, and by Thursday he could tell the time had come.

That night after supper, in quiet, cautious excitement, Sam led her across the river, the while hoping The Red Duke would not cause a commotion. Unless it had been a long time since he'd been used, it was unlikely that he'd wreck his pen, for that had never been essential to fulfillment before. If only he didn't get excited and start bellowing.

There was a half-moon and a starry sky. Every once in a while Sam would pause and listen for the movement of anyone who might have had occasion to stay at the big bull's pen. There was no sound. Twice the cow started to bawl, but each time Sam kicked her so smartly in the belly that she stopped.

Then they were at the pen and there was The Red Duke, a mammoth maroon-and-white creature, weighing a ton and more, his great dewlap swinging like a pendulum whenever he moved his short, thick forelegs. You could have rolled a sirup bucket from his head down his square neck and back to his tail without its once falling off.

Quickly Sam opened the gate, ushered in his palpitant charge, and waited.

The Red Duke only stood there. He was detached and moody. This was nothing either new or rare to him. He had only half turned his head as the cow entered the pen.

"Well, God dog," Sam murmured, impatient, nervous, continually looking back over his shoulder.

The Red Duke picked up a wisp of straw, chewed it absently, spat it out. To Sam, he had become considerably less beautiful.

The cow snuggled to the bull's side.

Sam was pleased with the interest she was taking and the effort she was making. But it seemed futile.

Sam heard a car coming down the road. It might very well be one of Harley Murphy's men. Quickly he put the rope around the cow's neck, but just as quickly The Red Duke seemed to understand it was now or never. He was a different animal, suddenly rearing mightily into the air. Now his great mass was more shocking than ever. It was incredible that two legs could hold that terrific weight. And yet he was almost deft as, with one Jovian thrust that Sam knew instantly was sufficient, he sent Uncle Walter sprawling onto the ground in a kind of sublime astonishment.

At the same time the car on the road had stopped at the barbed-wire gap. A man was getting out to open it. Frantically Sam tugged at the now lackadaisical cow, trying to get her off the ground. Finally, by twisting her tail, he got her on her feet and out of the pen.

As the man got into the car to drive through, Sam was dragging the still dreamy, almost inert cow across the pasture toward the river. He saw it was too late to avoid the momentary flash of headlights as the car made a turn in the lane. He darted back and hid behind the cow, hoping breathlessly that the driver would not notice Uncle Walter among the other cows.

On the car came, the lights beginning to swing around. What criminal statute, Sam wondered, would cover this case? The beam of light fell on the cow. Sam held his breath and kept his body low. But the moment the lights were off them, Sam crouched in front of Uncle Walter and dragged her on. Ten minutes later they reached the protective growth of tall blood-weeds along the river and were safe.

At the pole-pen, in a sweat of relief, Sam put the cow

inside and struck a match. In Uncle Walter's back there was a telltale kink. He patted her neck and closed the gate.

Walking on home, illuminated by the thought of what a splendid calf Uncle Walter was now in the process of having, Sam was not without a certain nagging little sense of guilt, a feeling of having stolen something that was not a necessity. He was surprised, since he'd had no fore-warning of it while contemplating this foray. Actually he felt a little tricked. His instincts had given him the go-ahead sign and then allowed his conscience to hurt him.

But by the next morning, when he told his secret to old man Hewitt, he had figured the thing out and his conscience was at rest.

"Harley's got more good high-bred bulls than his cows can use up," Sam said. "It never cost him an extra penny or anything he could of used hisself. I figger it was just like swipin a ride on the train. It's goin where it's goin anyhow, and if you can't afford a ticket, the company ain't goin to be any richer whether you swipe a ride or whether you walk."

"Anyhow," the old man said, "it ain't nothin you can very well carry back, so I guess we might as well get on with our plowin."

21

As the fields began slowly to be starred with white locks of cotton, Sam went to Ruston and asked, "Do you expect me to pick that cotton at six bits a day?"

"Of course not," Ruston said. "I expect to pay you four bits a hundred, just like I would anybody else. You won't even have to weigh it in the field. Just go by gin weights. And take after that part on the overflow land like you had a blow-torch on your tail. Give er one more round of poison, though. That'll last another week or so, and by that time she'll be popped wide open. If the leaf worms want to strip er then, let em strip."

Sam was in the lower field next day, poisoning, when the school bus stopped at the crossroads. Daisy had been to a meeting at the Hackberry public school, which as yet had not opened for the fall term. The County Home Demonstration Agent had summoned all the rural children in the district.

Knowing Daisy would want to report on her trip before going to the house, Sam stopped at the turn-row and rolled a cigarette, watching her scramble duck-leggedly out of the bus and come flying toward him.

"Lemme ride," she said when she came up to him.

"Get over on the other side out of that poison," Sam said. "You'll be snuffin it up your nose and the next you know there won't be no Daisy."

"All right," she said, obeying. "Now let me on."

"You done had your ride on that nice school bus," Sam said. "What'd they tell you at the meetin?"

"What's been wrong with Jot and all the rest of us every spring. What Granpa and Aunt Nettie died of."

"Aw!" he said.

"They did."

"What did they call it?"

"Said it was pellagra."

"But they never knowed Granpa nur sister Nettie, neither."

Thereupon, remembering hard, Daisy told him all the symptoms, how it began by skin sores brought out by the spring sun, that it was caused by living on cornbread, salt pork, and molasses throughout the winter. And this year the school was putting on a campaign to persuade its country patrons to balance their diet for the coming winter.

This worried Sam.

"How you gonna eat somethin you ain't got?" he asked. "Did they tell you that, too?"

"Uh huh. They said raise a fall garden and put stuff up in jars, and when winter came you'd have it."

Sam was impressed. Actually this conversation was bringing to a head a matter to which he'd given considerable thought throughout the summer. Dr. White had made it clear that the old diet amounted to a kind of slow starvation, and yet fall gardening and cotton-picking stood squarely in each other's way. And cotton-picking time was when you made the handful of money that was going to have to carry you through the winter. But Daisy's report made indecision no longer possible. It had lighted a path through the future that you could abandon only with complete assurance that disaster was certain. It seemed odd, actually, that he had not thought it out before.

"Now see there, Sister, what you've gone an learnt," Sam said. "It's wonderful, ain't it! Just to think, turnip greens ain't only just pore folks' fodder, but kinda like medicine that you take in advance."

"That's what they said."

"Well, Sister, your daddy ain't never goin to let you nor Jot nor Mamma ever have no more spring sickness. We're gonna garden while the gardenin's good, and come by them glass jars somehow."

Daisy was immensely proud that her news was considered so important.

"I'm gonna run tell Mamma," she said, and sailed across the field toward the house.

For a moment Sam stood there, still benumbed by the shocking simplicity of mastering a lifelong dread. Not only was there a way now to cure spring sickness; there was a way to forestall it. And as he took off his shoes and dumped the accumulated clods out on the ground, he felt a lonesomeness for knowledge, the thing that made old fears vanish and told a man how to do things, what to worry about and what not to. More than ever he realized there were two worlds, a light one and a dark one, and sensed that his was full not only of real but imaginary troubles, and that he was helpless to tell which was which.

Slightly saddened, he re-lit his cigarette and felt better. He meant to relay to old man Hewitt all that Daisy had said. It was sense and therefore would be welcome to the old man.

He tossed a clod at Weaver's rump that put him back in motion.

That night he discussed it with Nona.

"I reckon the school folks're bound to know," Nona said, "but it couldn't hardly have come at a worse time. I mean with all this cotton to pick."

Sam was lying comfortably barefooted on the bed.

"Looks like don't nothin come handy farmin," he said, "and it shore don't come twicet. We just got to do it anyhow. This what Daisy's learnt ain't just a big thing. It's a *great* big thing. We got a winter to make, and if we've got stuff put up we'll have took the main money strain off of ourselves. But where it comes in mostly, is we'll be preventin spring sickness."

Granny did not take the least stock in the medicinal

value of this proposal, but a mess of stringbeans any time you wanted it did not require any special recommendation as far as she was concerned.

"You're right, Sammy boy," she said. "You got a head on you like a tack."

"I spec them jars'll be pretty high," Nona said. "I know we'll have our pickin money, but nobody's got any good shoes sides me and we ought to have two sets of long drawers apiece to make the winter on."

"Just have to manage, I guess," Sam said. "What's botherin me is gettin the garden land broke. Soon as I get through poisonin, he'll send for the mules."

"You don't use but one to the poisoner," Nona said. "I'll take the other one and break the garden while you finish poisonin. It wants to be broke light, anyhow, don't it?"

"That's right."

"How much ought we to get ready?"

Sam thought.

"Would two acres seem crazy?"

"That's a heap o garden. Especially to buy jars for."

"Let's risk it," Sam said. "I mean if you feel like gettin that much ready."

Nona nodded. It was marvelous the way she nodded, as if before the will of God. Who else had a woman like that?

"Tween us," Sam said proudly, affectionately, "we get a lot done."

Nona did not look up.

"In just about a minute," Granny said, "I guess the

blanket'll go up on the wall and me and the kids'll get run out on the porch."

Sam laughed. It would have suited him. He was at peace, and pervaded by the splendid truth that now he and Nona were going to raise a crop which would be theirs entirely. It would not be sold for money but would bring health and strength to their own family. No matter how you cared to look at it, it was a wonderful thing to do.

Granny sat in her chair chuckling over her joke.

Nona went out behind the house, among the dead corn stalks, and lay on the ground and sobbed, and her hands dug into the black earth.

In the house she had felt almost a supernatural unity with her family, an inner radiance created by Sam's affection and respect, and the old woman had defiled it. You couldn't kill her, and God was too mean to take her away, and she'd never stop suffocating you with her presence, never stop quirting you with her voice. The few moments when the poverty-stricken may know a little dignity and feel a little cleanliness behind the walls of their own hovels, even this was denied to her. And she sobbed her sorrow, her utter despair, into the earth.

Then she got up and dried her eyes, and the south wind blew on them.

When she went back into the house, Sam asked, "Where you been?"

"Just out," Nona said, and began making down the children's pallet on the floor.

22

THREE days later the poisoning was finished and the garden ready for planting. Then Ruston came.

"Sam," he said, "I been thinking about that bottom cotton. We got to snatch it out of there before the weather gets bad. I'll send a truckload of hands, and the truck can haul the cotton. I'll leave the hill cotton for you and your wife to pick, and when that's done you can come to the big place and go on picking."

"It'd been handier for me the other way," Sam said, "but this way makes more sense. Send em on."

And the next day they came. There were some white people in the truck, and a few Mexicans, but most of them were Negroes, and the Negroes were the music.

All year they had been doing other things, separately mostly, and not making a living, certainly not picking cotton. This was the season of festival, when there were money and work and others of your kind working all about you. If you were young, it was an opportunity for love, for sly, loud courtship; if you were old, for reunion. And there was still a tribal thing in your blood which said that in numbers, in hot, loud numbers, there were well-being and relaxation and joy.

Now the air was full of banter, of the live pungency of hot bodies stinking, of the sheen of smooth, black, sweaty skin over magnificent muscles, of a strange, latent yearning for the dead dream of emancipation, latent just now because it was cotton-picking time. But even picking time, which had always been yours and your people's, was each year becoming more diluted with Mexicans and poor whites. Yet there was still music at night, a little friggin, a little preachin. Nobody was a stranger. People chatted with you while you worked.

"Where y'all from?"

"Jest Hackberry."

"We's from Falls County."

"Sho nuff? We picked there in '36."

"Been here fore now, cep the Sociation was meetin."

"That's church, ain't it?"

"Kinda. We always meets at this time to get the repo'ts an for closin the physical year."

"Oh. This hyear cotton's real, ain't it? No bollies to it."

Sunbonnets. Knee pads made of old automobile casings.

"Fo bits a hunderd ain't much price, is it?"

"Law, chile, I seen it two dollars."

"That uz wahtime."

"Sposed to be one goin on somewhere now."

"Cross the waters, ain't it?"

"That's right. Who's that lady with the cute behind over there?"

"My sister Vashti, that's who."

"Oh. Scuse me."

A clear strong voice blasts out against the hot sky:

> *Me an my wife and my wife's frens*
> *Can pick mo cotton than the ginner can gin.*

Sixty hands. A bale picked every two hours. Seven hundred and fifty pounds of cotton with the seed in it gathered every sixty minutes. Four bales by two o'clock. That was when it began raining.

Sam didn't like it. This was a bad time for a rain to come. Fortunately it began slowly, with no wind, and the cotton had a chance to become thoroughly drenched, to reinforce its position in the boll with wetness, so that it would not be knocked out on the ground.

When Ruston's foreman saw the rain was something more than a shower, he loaded the last bale of picked cotton onto the truck and the Negroes on top of it and hauled them away.

A family of white migrant pickers, who had been hired to work until the bottom cotton was picked, remained. There were five in the family: a man, his wife, a grown son, and two children. All they had for protection against the rain was the bed of an old four-cylinder Chevrolet truck. The woman and children had already crawled underneath it, and the man and his son were arranging a ragged wagon sheet across the loaded truck bed.

Sam went over and, uninvited, began helping stretch the canvas. The man was big and heavy and his features and hands were rough from exposure and work. There was a kind of broad, direct force about him. His son was callow and vague in comparison.

"Where was you all aimin to spend the night?" Sam asked.

"Figured on campin."

"It ain't gonna be no night for that. We got a kind of old half-way room up at the house with one wall fell in. It ain't much better'n out here, but if you'd care to use it, more'n welcome."

"That's mighty nice," the man said. "Squat down here under the truck. I'll tell Hattie."

"Better load em up under that wagon sheet fast as you can," Sam said. "Much water soaks into the road, we ain't gonna be able to make the hill."

The man told Hattie, a wizened but hornety woman, who understood the urgency of getting started at once, and only nodded her sincere thanks to Sam and began putting the children into the truck.

Sam cranked the thing and climbed in beside the man.

When they started moving, the driver said, "My name's Tom Clampett. We sure preciate this favor."

Sam introduced himself, then said, "She's loaded a little heavy on your side, ain't she?"

"No, sir. The left side of the back spring busted a few days ago. She's ridin on the axle."

At the house Granny, who had been watching the approach of the truck, was in a frenzy.

"Lord save us!" she said in dancing, fluttering excitement. "He's bringin a whole wagonload of folks! They'll eat us out o house n home!"

"Don't talk so loud," Nona said.

When Sam came in, he said, "Some folks are spendin the night in the other room. They got rained offen the road."

"They a-eatin supper here?" Granny asked.

Sam looked at Nona.

"We can give em coffee and bread, can't we?" he asked.

"That ain't much company supper," she said.

"Well, beggars can't be choosers," Granny said. "They got to take what's in the trought."

Sam cut his eyes at her.

"That's enough of that," he said. "These is nice folks. They're our company."

"I never meant nothin," Granny said. "Reckon I'm just excited. What I said's the truth, though. But I'm glad they came."

Nona went over and picked up the sirup can and shook it.

"Sposin I made a couple o molasses pies," she said. "We've got enough to make two kinda thin ones."

"Now you done it," Sam said happily. "You done made somethin out of this supper thing. Them folks'll really enjoy hot bread and coffee an pie. Why, you couldn't hardly beat that nowhere."

"Where's the kids?" Nona asked, to cover her pleasure.

"Law, they ain't took their eyes off the visitin folks," Granny said. "They're in there gettin quainted."

Sam went to the door and called, "You folks come in when you're ready. I'll get a fire goin here in the fireplace."

The door opened and the woman came in.

"I'm Mrs. Clampett," she said. "This is sure nice of you all."

"Just tickled to have you," Sam said. "This is my wife, Nona, and this is Granny."

Nona gave Mrs. Clampett a shy, humble smile of welcome.

"Take a seat here in my rocker," Granny said with the air of a person who was unconcernedly giving away a two-story house.

"F you'll scuse me," Nona said, embarrassed, "I'll get on with my work. I'm fixin to stir us all up some bread."

"Oh, we ain't goin to eat up you folks' supper," Mrs. Clampett said. "We're grateful for the use of your roof."

Someone had to persuade Mrs. Clampett that the Tuckers wanted them, and Nona, to whom she had been speaking, didn't know how. She looked pleadingly at Sam.

"You all just got to," Sam said. "Such as it is, we got plenty."

Then Tom Clampett came in. His hair was combed, and he was wearing a clean, dry jumper. He had an armload of the wood which was stored in the west room.

"I brought a little wood for that far you was talkin about," he said to Sam. "Like for me to build it?"

"No, sir," Sam said. "Have er goin in a minute. Take a seat if you can find a dry place. That's Nona and Granny. Where're you folks from?"

"Well," Tom Clampett said, "we come from about twenty miles east of Hackberry. But we come by way of California."

"Mercy," Sam said hostily, happily, delighted with himself and Nona and the company and the pies Nona was going to make.

By now the rest of the Clampetts, with Jot and Daisy at their heels, had sifted into the room.

"I tell you we've seen a heap o stuff since we left this country," Mrs. Clampett said. "Seen a heap more'n I ever want to see again."

"We was in the big strike," Tom said, rolling a half-length cigarette from Sam's offered can. "Things came pretty hard on us."

"Them folks are mean out there," Mrs. Clampett said. "Just pure dee mean."

"We was mean too," Tom said, moving out from under a leak that was beginning to drip on his left shoulder. "It wasn't no playin school. It was a strike."

"They run us out of places where we weren't doin nothin," Mrs. Clampett said. "Some vigilantes caught Theodore and beat him up."

Tom Clampett pointed at the young man who was sitting on the pile of wood behind Sam. "That's Thee," Tom said. "Thee ain't practical. He talked when he ought to been listenin. I done in some scabs and got away. But Thee never done nothin but some talkin and he got beat up."

"I don't keer," Thee said. "I taken a lickin, but I seen somethin. I don't have to strike no more. I done caught on."

"Thee aimed to make a preacher," Tom said. "Then he talked to so many of them Reds that he commenced preachin that."

"Not no more, though," Thee said. "I done had the vision. Hit's too late for strikin. The ball's done started rollin an nothin's gonna stop it this side of home plate."

"Maybe Mr. Tucker ain't intrested in that stuff," Tom said tentatively, treating neither Sam nor Thee with disrespect.

"I ain't got it just straight in my mind," Sam said, "what it is that's got rollin."

"Hit's organizin that's got started," Thee said, with a moving intensity. "I commenced preachin Jesus and the brotherhood of man and then I seen how things was and mixed it up kinda with Communism. They got some good in that stuff. They got the spirit strong, but it's a hatin spirit. And I knowed that was wrong and it worried me. Done a heap o prayin and says, 'Jesus, I mean to do my best, but it ain't all addin up. I done put in with the poor and downtrodden and the new disciples, and they don't study nothin but raisin hell.' But that time I didn't get no answer.

"Then after we'd done left California, these new disciples just hauled off an joined up with the enemy. I mean their Boss Man did, and there most of em was, brokenhearted and double-crossed. They'd give up everthing for this here new road to salvation, and it turned out that a Judas was runnin the thing. And I knowed there wasn't nothin to do in all this confusion cept to buckle down an pray.

"Happened I was in the Roswell jail for vag. Prayed two days and never et a bite. Me there in that jailhouse just a-prayin and a-fastin, and that second night I seen it: how everbody was organizin. Everbody was sayin we got to organize to get anything done. The pore and the rich. Even the stores organizin into chains. Don't nobody hardly know what to do no more less they're organized. People just gets lonesome and feels helpless and so they organize. It's done got started and can't stop, just eatin up folks like a hay-baler eatin Johnson grass. Folks acrost the waters is gettin organized by the sword—and us by the light which we got to hold up in a darkenin world.

"I seen Armageddon was comin on.

" 'Jesus,' I says, 'You done it by meekness an love. That was Your power. But I don't see how it's gonna stop the cannon of the new Philistines.'

" 'That ain't what I done when the money changers defiled the temple,' He says. Says, 'I taken Me a rawhide whip and stood up for what I knowed was right.' Says, 'I was all by Myself but I got the job done.'

"Says, 'Walk among My people, Thee, with humility and love, but rise against whatever would oppress them.' Says, 'Go among em, and tell em this: that they got two great enemies. They know the tyrant is their enemy, but they can whup him, if they can handle the other one.'

" 'What is that other'n, Jesus?' I ast Im.

"An He says, 'It's a thing My people carry in themselves, a thing every man totes in his bosom. It's a little voice that whispers to you in the black of night and says, "Ain't no use to try so hard. Ain't no use to give so much out of yourself in the good fight. Look at your comrades. They ain't tryin hard as you." An when you've listened to that, it says, "Feller, you're tired. You're played out." Says, "There ain't no use to struggle any longer," an this voice is gettin sweeter an more convincin, and then it says, "Why, you ain't fightin for nothin but a little old idea. An it's out of date. Freedom ain't nothin much. Nur brotherhood neither." Says, "Feller, you're *awful* tired. Your arm is weak and your sword ain't sharp." Then it kisses your ear and whispers, "Surrender."

" 'That's the great enemy,' He says. 'It's the voice of death. The voice of life says struggle and strive, says take risks and shoot the works and don't study nothin but winnin the good fight. That there courage-sappin voice of death is the hidden friend of the tyrant. Now, Thee, you go forth and tell My people,' He says. 'Tell what I just said and give em My promise, which I here solemnly make to them. If the last one of em is put to the sword, the light won't fail. Whatever brute and killer holds the power of Caesar, the light won't die in men's hearts, cause it's one of those things that burns brighter under pressure.' Says, 'You seen how it burnt in the early Christians. Well, when the new Caesar puts the screws on again, she'll brighten up. And a heap o hearts that didn't know they had courage in em'll have it then.

" 'So tell My folks to go into battle with their tails up an their convictions strong, like I went when they nailed Me up on that cross.' Says, 'Them boys rubbed Me out, but the light just got stronger.'

" 'But, Jesus,' I said, 'won't this here fightin talk make the people mean? Won't it poison their hearts with hatred?'

"An then this little ole Jesus with the scraggly beard and the big warm eyes looked at me and says, 'No, Theodore.' Says, 'I love the meek and pore and the generally no count. But there's somethin else I love too. Somethin that brings a mist to My eyes and a shine to My heart.'

"I said, 'What's that?'

"An He says, 'A man with love in his heart and guts in his belly.' Says, 'You can look the wide world over an you won't find nothin better.' Says, 'If there's any substitute for a brave, decent man, I don't know what it is.'

" 'Arm My people, Theodore, and arm em with swords that'll cut. Then when the time comes, go lead em.' Says, 'Make their hearts throb with the spirit of brotherhood so they'll spring to the conflict, not in hate of men but lovin em, not greedy for conquest but glad to sacrifice themselves for the freedom of all men.' Says, 'Lead em into that fray with a song on their lips and their eyes bright with the awful light of hell.' Says, 'Keep on leadin em, Theodore, the livin marchin over the dead, till My people, till all people, is free and safe, till a world's made that's big enough to hold generosity and love.' "

Thee paused and dropped his eyes, conscious for the first time of how long he'd been talking. Outside, the rain fell steadily. Now a thin, six-inch band of water was exploring a path down the front of the chimney.

"That's what I seen," Thee said, "that second night in the jailhouse when I was fastin and prayin."

"Well, that was sure somethin to see," Sam said.

"I've studied on this vision of Thee's a right smart," Tom Clampett said, "an to my way of thinkin, it kind of adds up to somethin."

"I really seen it," Thee said, "and He told me all them things."

"I ain't doubtin it," Sam said. "I've always figgered that the difference tween a good man and a cull was whether he'd stand up for what he thought was right. . . . What you gonna do about your vision, Thee?"

"Tell it," Thee said. "I'm gonna tell it everwhere I go, an I ain't ever gonna stop goin."

"An he will too," Tom said. "Thee may not be much to look at, but he's got the spirit strong. Fact of the matter, he's got right smart little guts."

One of the Clampett girls and Daisy came around passing plates.

"We got to eat in the spots where the roof's not leakin," Nona said. "There ain't one big enough for the table."

Sam had been completely carried away by Thee's passionate account of his vision, but now he suddenly remembered he was these people's host.

"Here," he said, passing his plate to big Tom. "This ain't very heavy but"—he knew he shouldn't tell but had already started and, blushing with embarrassed pride, added, "we got pie comin."

It rained all night and when morning came it still fell, evenly, the leaks still splattering on the sodden floor. The Clampetts had meal and could not be prevented from furnishing the breakfast bread. They also had a pound of sugar for the last of the coffee.

Late that afternoon the river started up into the sloughs, and the drenched men netted a whopping buffalo. But the families ate it soberly, without jollification. The river was rising. The bottoms were lavish with cotton. Except to pick, it was not theirs, but they were all cotton people, knew what every pound of it had taken out of some man and some mule. No matter what the market said it was worth, they knew.

That night, when the rain did not abate, Sam brought the cow and the calf out of the bottoms.

The third morning came and the rain still fell without increase or decrease. Sam saw his neighbors walking through the mud to the brow of the hill, and he and Tom and Thee went out into the rain to watch beside them.

Below and beyond them through the tree trunks on the banks they saw the yellow river slowly bulging toward the tall, ripe cotton which hung limp against the bosom of the valley. There was easily a bale to the acre and it shone brightly against the wet black earth. The sky was a low series of bending gray curtains shredding off into rain, bringing the horizons almost within a stone's throw. The men on the hill were isolated in the small, dimly visible area around them that seemed to hold all the light remaining on earth. Quietly they stood there, the rain drumming an unvarying cadence on their black hats, streaming down their red necks, their numb, insensible faces.

Somewhere in the valley a calf bawled, frightened, pleading. The river was slipping out of its banks now, striping the furrowed fields with yellow. The men stood, drenched and somberly watching.

The rain fell.

23

WHEN the river receded, there was a silence in the bottoms that had not been there before. Shapes were suspended awkwardly in new, as yet unassimilated, death. The felt sound and motion of growing cotton, which had until now gone unnoticed, were no longer there. The substance of thousands of shirts and trousers, of sheets and jumpers and socks, of warm, knit drawers that might have been worn against the cold, had gone down the river or was rotting in mud.

But once you got it through your head and felt its utter spoliation and that nothing could bring it back, it was just another disaster that had happened in what was already the past, another disaster that had left you in a hell of a mess but that you would live through.

The Clampetts had stayed an extra day after the rain stopped, working on the broken spring, and then had gone on down the road looking for hill cotton to pick. Now you waited for the ground to dry, to pick what was left of your own hill cotton, the little that the rain had not rotted in the boll—and to plant your garden, because it alone must stand you through the winter. It and your wits and courage. For when the last of the cotton was picked, your job was over. You had served your term of usefulness to Ruston. You might stay, rent free, in that worse than makeshift house. But the crop was made. You were on your own with no capital whatever.

After Sam settled up with Ruston, he and Nona held council. The two pairs of long underwear for each of the family had to be bought. That was absolutely the cheapest way to make winter clothes out of summer ones. Daisy had to have a pair of stout shoes for school. For the rest, rubber glue-on half-soles must serve. They could be bought for thirteen cents a pair. The rest could also do without stockings, but Daisy ought to have some cotton ones for cold weather: all this and food and garden seeds and plants had to come out of eight dollars and forty cents. This would be the last real money they would see.

"What about the jars?" Nona asked.

"We'll have to get em some other way," Sam said. "I'll do some work for somebody. I just wisht we was able to get somethin pretty for you. Even if it wasn't anything but some little ole knickknack."

"I still got them nice stockins," she said. "If we had money to spend, we'd have to buy a new skillet. There's

a hole come in the old one, but I use it tiltin and don't
waste much grease."

A kind of sickness came over Sam.

"God, we're pore," he said. "Sometimes I forget."

For a moment they sat staring at this fact, so old it was
usually taken for granted.

"It don't differ," Nona said wanly, not knowing the
uncrushable listlessness she conveyed to Sam. "We'll make
out. We always do."

"When we get rich," Granny said, then re-phrased it
to: "when our ship comes in, I want us to get one of them
talkin machines and a lot of good sacred records. I want
to set on the gallery and drink lemonade with ice in it,
and hear 'Beulah Land.' Says:

> *"I'm drinkin at a fountain*
> *Underneath a cloudless sky,*
> *Praise God,*
> *I'm drin-kin at a foun-tane*
> *That ne-ver shall run dry,*
> *Hallelujah! . . ."*

She was lost in song and pleasant images.

"Better add a pound of Epsom salts," Nona said. "It
ain't but a dime n'll last us."

These things were bought and stored and Sam began
planting potatoes. Then peas and beans and carrots, cabbage for kraut, garlic to be plaited into ropes to dry, beets,
onions, turnips, even a nickel pack of lettuce seeds.

Nona helped. In a week it was done. And it was still
September. There need be no frost until late November.

If the yield was good, no reasonable number of fruit jars could hold it.

For the next couple of weeks, Sam realized, Nona could take care of the garden. He should be out earning something. Where? Locally there was no cotton to pick. West Texas? That Never-Never Land?

You saw your friends and asked about people.

"Oh, they gone off cotton-pickin. T' West Texas."

Was everybody in creation needed to pick cotton in West Texas? He didn't think so. There was no use getting separated from the family on any wild-goose chase, on any profitless picnic to West Texas.

You were a good hand to butcher, but it was still burning summer weather. Too early for people even to think of killing hogs.

Of course if you could catch old Lead and get even a nickel a pound for him in nigger town. . . . And yet that was a long chance, to be taken half for the sport of it.

No use going down Mamma's way. Sandy-land folks would pick what cotton they raised their ownself. Or be cuttin cane and . . . Well, hell. There it was, plain as the nose on your face.

It was sirup-makin time and when you was known to be a sirup-cookin dude . . . Specially when you'd take your pay in sirup, if you couldn't get money. . . . Anyway, it would be better than sittin here doin nothin.

He went to tell Nona he was going.

In town Sam asked Russell if he knew who had some ripe cane, and Russell said Tiff Mosely.

"I wanted to help make sirup," Sam said, "but he's got all them old boys."

"They aren't any count, though," Russell said. "Go on down there."

Tiff was a whisky-and-fiddle-music man. He was the leader of a little neighborhood string-music-and-holler band, had moonshined all his life, and was, no doubt, still at it. When Sam walked up to Tiff's place, he saw Tiff down in a post oak grove below the house by the cane crusher and sirup vat.

"Come on and enter in," Tiff said. "We're fixin to run off a few sirup."

"I came lookin for a cookin job," Sam said. "I never burnt up a batch of sirup in my life."

"Well, we got a yardful of hands now," Tiff said. "It might throw us off balance if one of em was any good."

The boys looked good-naturedly amused.

"Couple o gallons of sirup a day an what I'd eat'd be pay enough," Sam said. "I been known to give sirup a mighty fine flavor."

"All right," Tiff said, "take charge. You boys get to haulin an runnin the crusher."

The work began. Loads of cane were coming in. Sam got his fire going under the vat. Round and round, dreamily, almost asleep, a bay mule walked at the end of the crusher pole, supplying the mill with power. And it was both peaceful and exciting, working with these sand people, getting all the sand news, hearing how each old acquaintance had made out with his crop, with his family and neighbors. Hearing who had held house dances, who had fought whom, and who had done the diddling. Just keep your fire going easy and slow, and the scum skimmed off the juice.

About five o'clock Tiff went off somewhere and came back with a jug of whisky and a bucket of water. And that was the last of sobriety for the duration of the sirup making.

Tiff's orchestra was playing that night and they took Sam along. The dance was to be at Uncle Billy Harrington's house, which by eight o'clock was packed literally to capacity, and the stomp of feet drowned out the string music for all but the musicians themselves, which was as it should be; drowned out everything in fact but the hollering of the host; and the old house quivered and breathed with each beat.

"Go on and dance er off the God blumbed blocks!" Uncle Billy yelled. "Dance er to the ground. Man's gonna lose his house, there ain't no better way."

"You fixin to lose it, Uncle Billy?" somebody asked.

"Hit's fixin to lose me!" he yelled cheerfully. "Done come seventy and raised hell all my life. Fixin to go to Glory and when I get there I'm gonna holler."

It was ten o'clock before the moon came up, and when it did Sam yielded to an old dance-party habit and went outside. With his sharp Indian eyes, he carefully surveyed the grassy hilltop where the dew was beginning to fall, watching for little glints of moonlight on dew-frosted glass. When the moon came up over the horizon was the time, had always been the time, to spot hidden whisky in the weeds. It wasn't stealing. It was just finding and taking. By unwritten, but mutually respected, law, there was always open season on hidden whisky. It was part of the adventure of a dance. Sam found a fruit jar full and a store-bought quart. But for old time's sake, he did his drinking from the home-made contents of the fruit jar.

Then later in the evening Runcie Melhorn's husband went off to the woods with a neighbor woman and Runcie told Sam, "I'm just a mind to give him a dose of his own medicine. What's fair for the gander is fair for the goose."

Runcie was not much to look at, but she was ready, and Sam was drunk. But before he said anything, he realized something: that accepting Runcie's invitation was not a question of violating his loyalty to Nona, but of making a cheap, insincere gesture. This was a dance, and would be, certainly, improved by a little diddling. Those things just went together. But it was Nona he wanted tonight: Nona, who was even less attractive than Runcie. In squiring Runcie to the nearest thicket, he would not be going behind Nona's back to steal a moment's pleasure. He'd be doing something he didn't actually want to do. If he did, it would be out of male habit and pretense, a mere ritualistic obeisance to the great virile concept of fornication. His loyalty to Nona was not an obligation, but, just now at least, an encompassing fact. To go outside and give Runcie a good genteel going over would be wrong, because it was not honestly what he wanted to do.

"Runcie," Sam said, full of a wild desire to laugh out loud at the pious fraud of what he was saying, "two wrongs don't make a right. If Meriweather wants to act like a God damned billy-goat, I guess it can't be helped."

With a slight, bogusly righteous nod, he left her, went outside, and took another drink.

The music sawed on gingerly. By now most of the celebrants were drunk, and the next thing Sam knew, a fight had started. He didn't know how, but saw it had and felt it growing, saw people adding themselves to it, helplessly, joyously, like a Saturday crowd converging on a medicine show. Everything was grunts and action, elbows and fists. The sharp report of country fist on skull was like the sound of a plank striking a stack of green cowhides. On dodging heads and plummeting fists, there was hot red blood. And Sam found himself full of a leaping desire to smack somebody, to slam the somersaulting Jesus out of somebody. But he was caught in a pocket of women who were shrieking in ecstatic horror, and there was nobody in reach besides Tiff standing there yelling, holding his fiddle in the air. Sam felt particularly warm toward Tiff, who had taken him in and entertained him so royally. The feeling, in fact, had by now become, in this by-whisky-exaggerated world, a high, burning comradeship. But Sam just had to smack somebody and there was nobody but Tiff, so he let him have it on the unsuspecting jaw.

It was marvelous. The arm and shoulder that had done it felt golden. A ball bat wouldn't have done it any better. Then a great crashing force struck Sam in the back of the head, and as he went down, in the last instant of fading consciousness, he saw Runcie standing over him with a chair leg in her hand, on her face a look of profound fulfillment.

Next morning late, the sirup mill was back in production, and everyone felt physically awful, but spiritually refreshed, and the complaints of their bodies were soon quieted with aspirin and whisky.

By the end of the third day the sirup had all been made and jugged. Nevertheless, Sam spent one more night with the Moselys. After breakfast the next morning, Tiff hitched the team and took Sam and his five gallons of sirup, which had been put up in an oil can, to town.

It had been a splendid interval, and Sam was now ready to work in the garden in earnest, in detailed seriousness. "I sure had a good time," he told Tiff as they parted in town, "and I really preciate it."

"Come back next year," Tiff said. "It won't never be that good again. But we can try, anyhow."

When Sam got home with the sirup, the wherewithal for a fabulous number of molasses pies, everybody was heartened, not only by this material aggrandizement, but by the further indorsement of the belief that when Sam went off he usually brought back something good and valuable. But as much as anything, they were glad that he was home.

When Granny had seen him coming up the road with the big can in his hand, she had hurriedly got herself a piece of bread and a saucer, but she was so delighted with Sam's homecoming that for a good quarter-hour she forgot to sample the sirup.

Already the cabbage plants and onion sets had taken hold and were growing. In no time now the whole patch would be striped with young plants pushing out of the earth. While Sam and Nona were out looking at the garden, she said, "Henry Devers wants to see you."

"What about?"

"The well rope broke."

Sam felt a flush of anger.

"All right," he said. "I'll go see him."

Sam went to Henry's house and called, "Hello."

Henry came out.

"Well," Henry said, with a strange, half-suppressed belligerency, "it broke."

"That's what Nona said."

"Well?"

"Let's look at it."

"I got it tied together," Henry said. "It won't run through the pulley no more. We have to draw hand over hand."

Sam looked at the threadbare rope.

"I got a little piece of calf rope over at the house," he said. "I believe I can splice it in and we could take out this wore-outest part."

"It's *all* wore out," Henry said.

"But I nelly know I could make it work," Sam said.

"That wasn't our trade," Henry said. "We said when it was wore out, you'd get a new one."

"But all we want is to get the water up," Sam said. "The rope ain't got nothin to do with the taste."

Henry's hand slipped into his knife pocket.

"You lible to be gone fore long," he said. "You'll be asselin over the country day-laborin. You've wore out

my rope drawin my water and now you want to nigger
on your trade."

"Henry, I ain't got any money."

"That ain't none of my business. You owe me a well
rope and I want it."

"Would you take a gallon of home-made sirup in place
of it?"

"Sirup won't draw no water."

"I'll see what I can do," Sam said. "I'll take my sirup to
town and swap it for a rope. Unless"—he looked into
Henry's eyes, no longer trying to hide from Henry the
fact that he was beneath contempt—"unless you mean to
eat me up blood-raw lessen I just squat down here and
give birth to a well rope."

"All I want's the rope. If it takes you a day to get it,
I'll put up with that."

"I'm gonna get it," Sam said. "But you don't have to
put up with nothin from me. All you got to do any time
is just hop on me. I'm a man hates neighbor-fightin, but
you've bout got me lookin forward to the time when you
pull that little ole pocket knife out in the open."

Henry did not say anything.

Sam went home.

On the following day he traded two gallons of sirup
to the hardware man in town for a well rope, which he
brought home and strung through Henry's pulley. But
he was sick with shame at being thus swindled.

From the well he went to his own front porch, where
he sat a long while, thinking things over.

Now, to his left, the sun was going down in a nest of burnished clouds, sending tall columns of bright pink afterglow into the darkening sky. Flocks of doves, which had been feeding in the weed fields, were tracing flat trajectories across the September sky to the river to drink at its shallow edges and mourn softly, yearningly, to tell you that the world was full of sadness, that a little matter of a well rope was but a drop in man's ageless, oceanic sorrow, that soon night and sleep and peace would come. Gently they mourned for a sorrow that grew still more profound as night fell.

24

THERE were two ways of preserving the yield of the garden, of holding it fixed in freshness and usefulness throughout the winter. One was with glass jars, the other with tin cans. The jars cost the most, but might be used continuously, year after year. On the other hand, a pressure cooker was imperative if tin cans were used. Also there would have to be an apparatus for fixing the lids on the filled cans. Sam and Nona figured a long time, but in the end it looked as if glass jars were going to be the more reasonable solution. They cost seventy-five cents a dozen, the tops a penny each. Ten dozen would not be too many.

The garden was growing. All the forces necessary

to a decent diet through the winter had been set in motion, except getting the jars. Sam made the rounds of the neighborhood looking for work: a fence to repair, a barn to mend, a well to clean. In advance he'd known, almost, that nobody could afford the luxury of a paid hand. But he wanted to be certain. There was not much use trying to make it fishing just now because the signs were wrong. He decided to ask the road commissioner for a job, realizing it was nearly hopeless, because neither he nor any of his kinfolk could ever pay a poll tax. The commissioner would know that Sam could bring him no votes at all. Nevertheless, Sam asked for a road job. He was told they'd keep him in mind for later on. He looked in town for yard work. He tried to get on the section gang. He applied to the relief agency, and its rolls were full.

Discouraged, he went home and made a handful of dough bait and started to the buffalo hole, to fish and think. Just to sit there fishing, instead of doing nothing, would give him the feeling of being a going concern, of stealing the time to think, instead of sitting in a vacuum with the finger of necessity pointing thought-shatteringly in his face.

As he walked down the road from the house to the river, he was disconcerted a little by the finality with which the growing season, the working season, was over, and the way this time of year had of leaving you on your own hands.

At the river he walked across the little mule pasture, which was dense with an undergrowth of brambles, head-high blood-weeds, and cockle-burs. Overhead were the close-grown tops of pecans and elms and cottonwoods and willows. It was while he was making his way through this thicket that the keen, tough thorns of a prickly ash took hold of the side of his overalls and tore them from thigh to knee.

Somehow this assault was the last straw in a long line of refusals and disappointments. He almost wept, and would have, except that in the back of his mind the thought of a grown man doing such a thing was so ridiculous that he grinned.

"Big ole stand-up-in-the-road-and-bawl-for-butter-milk," he thought. "Pore ole Sam Tucker. He thinks he has a mighty hard time. Snagged his pants and bellowed like a cut shoat."

It was really very pleasant, sitting there on the ground seeing what a simpleton you almost were, watching the self-pity scurry out of view like a gopher running into his hole.

He made a half-length cigarette, which he did these days to postpone emptying his last can, and rubbed his scratched leg. He was licking the edge of the stubby cigarette when suddenly he took it away from his lips and said aloud, "Why, God damn my time! I don't notice nothin. Got to have my very britches snatched off fore I can see the nose on my own face."

He got up and started back to the house, still deriding himself good-naturedly, as he might an old friend, for his blindness. All the while, however, he was delighted with his own perspicacity.

At home he sewed up his trousers and started to Ruston's commissary, caught a ride, and was there by three o'clock. He saw Ruston listening to the cotton reports over the radio and sharpening his pocket knife on the bottom of his shoe.

"Come on back," Ruston said, "and have a chair."

Sam did.

"Mr. Ruston, you know that little ole mule pasture on the creek bank?"

"Yes."

"Remember how it's all overgrowed with brambles and ain't fit for nothin but rabbits and squirrels?"

"I know. But the mules can rest there and drink water. The pasture ain't no count, but the water's wet."

"It could be plumb good, though, if it was to be cleared."

"I might of known you was going to try to sell me something," Ruston said. "Everybody else does. Sam, I spec you're broke and need some way to make a little money. Well, that just makes two of us."

"I know you got overflowed on all the way around, Mr. Ruston, but this ain't goin to cost you nothin."

"How's that?" Ruston asked.

"There's a dozen or so good, big pecan trees in that little patch. Been a-growin there forever. Pecans never been gathered cause nobody but the squirrels could get to em. Well, I'm offerin to clear that patch, stack and burn the brush, just for what pecans falls off."

"Well, naturally," Ruston said, "nobody'd turn that

down in my place. I just hope it'll be half-way worth your trouble."

"I'm willin to tackle it," Sam said. "But you'll have to credit me for an ax file. Teeth all wore off of mine. Won't even do no good gummin any more."

"Till you start next year's crop," Ruston said pleasantly, "you haven't got any credit here at all. But I'm going to give you the file because I don't figure fifteen cents is much to pay for getting that land cleared."

Sam grinned.

"You're a hell of a feller," he said. "Give it here an I'll start home. I'm gonna commence clearin in the mornin."

By sunrise next day Sam was in the bottoms with his ax, hacking away at the tough undergrowth, having the old truth repeated to him that nothing wants to die. By noon it looked as if a wildcat had teethed on his gloveless hands and forearms, but there was a respectable space of cleared earth to show for his morning. At each stroke of the sharp ax a bush had fallen, except for those times when the fending branches sent the blade futilely into the ground. One by one the saplings fell, the elm, the box elder, the hackberry, one by one to be roughly trimmed and stacked.

The bramble bushes were the worst, with their roots barricaded inside a barbed entanglement. Soon, however, Sam cut and trimmed a long branch of hickory, leaving three stout prongs on the end. With this hickory pitchfork he was able to hold back the thorny vines so that the blade might reach their roots.

Clearing brush is punishing work, but it goes if you make it go, if you make the ax strokes mean something. And in this you are helped by knowing that you are making a good thing on the face of the earth, a thing that less thoughtful and energetic men have allowed sinfully to waste. When you are making a clean place where pecans may fall, you are invigorated by the knowledge that it has been a wet year, in which pecan trees wallow and strengthen themselves like hogs. And your labor is fruitful not only in its prime objective, but in its by-product of fuel. From these two acres will come a winter's wood supply, and you'll give a load to old man Hewitt for the use of his team in hauling the rest up on the hill.

Another by-product is the swamp rabbit you saw sitting under a hollow stump, that you crept up on and, with a deft thrust, caught in your bare right hand. Still another thing that has accrued to you is the rash on your sweaty skin, the prickly fire in your scratched arms wherever the blood-weeds have rubbed them.

Nona wanted to do the raking and burning, but Sam said, "You look out for the garden," and, still using the pronged branch for a pitchfork, piled the brush where the heat of its burning would not reach the pecan trees, and set it afire. And it was done. What had been a thicket two weeks ago had become a park.

Now the time had come to make a trade with Russell. All you had to do was say you were ready, and Russell would bid on what you had: a pile of scrap iron or a three-legged mule, a crop of watermelons hauled to town or still on the vine in the field.

Sam sent word in to Russell that he had a crop of nuts to sell on the tree.

The next day at one o'clock Russell drove up to Sam's house.

Sam came outside and said, "Lo, Russell."

He could see Russell's eyes slinking away from a re-examination of the appalling house in which the Tuckers lived. Sam could see Russell was ashamed to be caught looking at what might be an embarrassment to Sam. But with a sudden change of tactics that was characteristic of Russell, out of his old belief that frankness might be best, he said, "That's the worst house I ever saw."

"It sure is sorry," Sam said. "Want to see the pecans?"

"Yes. Get in."

As they rode down to the bottoms, Sam said, "What's new in town?"

"I don't know. What kind of pecans have you got?"

"Search me. They just growed there."

"Trees haven't been budded?"

"Not that I know of."

At the mule pasture Sam opened the gate and Russell drove the car inside, hitting a weed-covered stump with a force that Sam was sure had wrecked the car permanently.

Russell backed off of it, however, and got out. Then he began examining the big trees.

"This's been a good year for pecans," Sam said. "Them buggers'll make more than it looks like."

"You got it pretty clean," Russell said.

"I'm spectin that to show up in the price," Sam said. "I had to do a heap o cleanin to put that crop in reach of the pickers."

Russell stopped and looked at him.

"Does that make the God damned pecans worth any more? When I sell em, will I get anything extra for how neat you kept your orchard? Besides, you'd have had to cut winter wood *somewhere*, wouldn't you?"

"It'll make pickin easier, anyhow," Sam said, smiling inside himself. He liked Russell and it amused him to see that you couldn't get the best of him. However, Sam was full of suspense about the price. He really had no idea at all what to expect from Russell.

"I'm going to make you an offer," Russell said, "for the crop like it stands. If another overflow comes and catches the nuts on the ground, that's my hard luck. But if you think I'm not going to hold out that six dollars you owe me, you're crazy."

At least he was going to offer as much as six dollars, and, it began to appear, more. But how much more? Sam had been waiting two weeks to find out. He had to know now.

"What's your price?" he asked Russell.

Russell thought a moment longer.

"Seventeen dollars," he said.

Sam felt as if he'd come into a fat inheritance. He had hoped for ten, and had been prepared to argue Russell out of withholding more than two or three dollars on the old debt. Now he could pay Russell in full, have the cash for ten dozen jars and tops, and have two dollars and thirty cents left over.

"It's a trade," Sam said.

"Sure you're satisfied?" Russell asked.

"Plumb sure."

"Good-by," Russell said abruptly, jerking himself away from this talk with Sam, stung with a sudden necessity to be alone and moving.

"Watch out for stumps," Sam called.

Russell did not watch out at all, but with a strange, hurried, blind directness drove across the new-cleared ground to the road.

Seventeen dollars.

Sam had managed to have himself paid more than a dollar a day for cutting his own winter's wood. He started home directly to tell the family.

As he walked up the hill, he realized there were still a couple of days before time for the canning to start. In this interval he meant to go the God damnedest, most triumphal and deserved fishing that ever was. With enormous hooks and baits and a kind of tackle his imagination had devised during the space of a summer's Lead Pencil dreams.

Nona and the family had seen Russell drive out of the bottoms, had known his business there, and were all on the porch as Sam walked up to the house, and in the eyes of each of them was the clear question they were afraid to ask, "What did he say?"

Then they saw Sam was grinning almost boyishly and knew everything was fine and all right.

"Papa traded good!" Daisy shouted, and exuberantly, pretending her action to be only a physical expression of the family's triumph, slapped Jot on the back with both hands with such well-directed force that she knocked him off the low porch to land in a heap in the yard.

It hurt Jot, but the sense of jollification was so strong and general that he decided not to cry, and ran to lock his arms around his father's left thigh and ride back to the porch.

25

THAT was the story of the jars. The garden had its
story too. It had been planted and the seeds and onion
sets and cabbage plants had lain in the warm, provocative
earth while Sam had been gone on his sirup-making
junket. Then he had come home and there had been the
difficulty about the worn-out well rope. And not long
afterward, when the garden rows were pale green with
young plants, Henry Devers's cows had got out in the
night, and what their patient, hungry muzzles had missed
their splayed feet had crushed. The garden lay in total
ruin.

In utter desolation Sam drove the cows home and called
Henry.

"Hello, Sam."

"Come here, Henry."

"What for?"

"I want to show you something."

At the devastated garden, Sam explained why it had been planted in the first place and how much it meant to his family.

Henry was at a loss to know what tone to take. Though his stock had unquestionably done this damage, he hesitated to say he was sorry. To do so might seem a confession of guilt and responsibility which would be held against him.

Finally he said, "There's still plenty of time to replant."

"I ain't got money to buy any more seeds and stuff."

"That's sure too bad," Henry said.

"You don't want to offer to make it good?"

"I'm hard up too," Henry said. "After all, I never *turned* em out. This is what the law calls an act of God. And for that matter, you've more than been paid in well water for what your seed cost. Everybody expects to pay for water, less they got their own."

In an exhausted way, Sam thought of knocking Henry's teeth out, but realized he was not angry, that despair left no room for anger.

"I guess my bread and coffee is ready," Sam said and left.

As he walked home, he knew that this was the end of the garden dream, the dream he'd had of holding autumn in his hand throughout the winter. His money and his seed were spent. Nor had he any means of getting more.

By the time he looked for work, which he'd be long in finding, and earned money for the seeds, it would be too late.

When he got home, the bread was done and he sat down and looked at it.

"Well," he said, "it looks like we made a water-haul on our garden."

"Don't you figger there's still time to replant?" Nona asked.

"To replant what?"

"Seeds and cabbage plants and onions."

"If we had em," Sam said. "Only I don't see no way . . ."

"I got five pairs of new drawers wrapped up in a paper," Nona said. "That leaves us one pair apiece for the winter. You can take them others back to the store and trade em for seed."

Sam looked at her.

"We *got* to have drawers," he said. "Freeze if we don't."

"I don't see no choice," Nona said. "When we quit clawin after somethin to eat, we might as well give up. We don't never have no real choice."

"I guess that's right," Sam said, feeling a surge of pride in himself and Nona.

After eating a little of the bread, he picked up the bundle and started off. But at the door he came back and, saying nothing, since nothing need be said of his respect for and devotion to her, kissed Nona on the cheek.

As he left the house, he passed Granny on the front

porch where she was weeping broken-heartedly. She had tried to hide her extra pair of drawers but Nona had found and confiscated them.

"Goin on seventy-four," the old woman was sobbing. "Rheumatism gets worse every winter, and she comes and strips me naked down to my skin—that hellion does that to me, that heartless bugger. Father in heaven, take me away. I can't stand it no longer. I'm wore out."

Sam paused and gave her a pat on the shoulder.

"Poor Granny," he said. "You have hell, don't you?"

"Don't nobody know," she sobbed. "Don't nobody know but Jesus."

Rains fell at lucky times on this second planting, and Nona spent most of her days weeding, staking, pruning. The result was the inevitable one when, under these conditions, good seed comes to rest in fertile earth. It was a thrilling picture to behold.

Daisy was inexpressibly excited because the teacher had promised a blue ribbon to each child who could persuade its parents to preserve a hundred jars of garden vegetables. This ribbon, her father assured her, was now practically pinned on her dress.

In the meantime the mule pasture had been cleared, the pecan crop sold, and the jars bought and paid for. At last things were in hand, and Sam was going fishing in the two or three days before the canning should start. Within this period he meant to do one thing: catch old Lead Pencil. The signs were right, he had the time and some new ideas. He would almost have taken an even bet, had he anything to wager, that by canning time old Lead would have spent his last hour in the river.

He went to town to borrow some hooks from a garage man who went to the Coast every spring to fish for tarpon.

"I ain't goin to lose these hooks," he told the man, "cause I'm goin' to have em tied on something that can't be snapped."

"I don't know what that could be," the man said.

"I been rootin around in you all's junk pile and found these old inner tubes. They're goin to be my lines. I'll make my leader runnin down to the hook out of somethin real stout, but my trot line's gonna be made out of these tubes. He's gonna rear and pitch and raise hell, but that tube line is goin to give when he rears and take up when he pitches."

The garage man said he thought it would look funny but it might work. He let Sam have the hooks.

That afternoon Sam spent fishing with a pole and line for bait of decent size and caught two gaspergou weighing nearly a pound each, a half-pound white perch, and some small catfish.

By night he had his trot line rigged in a deep pocket where he'd lost less ingenious rigs before. Just at dark he raised it for a last look at this splendid array of baits that no small fry would molest and that Lead Pencil could never steal, for the leaders had been passed through the gill slits of the bait fish and the hook points through their backs. For old Lead, this would be one kill with strange consequences.

Sam went home to supper and was still eating when he heard some one outside calling hello.

He went to the door and said, "All right?"

"This is Henry, Sam. I'm gonna kill a hog Monday morning if it's cool enough, and want you to help me."

"That's mighty nice," Sam said. "But our garden's gonna commence coming in about Saturday and we're gonna try to can it up fast as it gets ripe. So I reckon that'll knock me out on the hog killin. Won't you come in and set?"

"No. I just came to ask you to help me butcher. It's the first thing I ever asked you and you ain't got time."

"No use to feel that way," Sam said. "I'd of done had the garden canned if your cows hadn't of et it up before."

"That's the way it goes," Henry said. "I'd meant to give you a good mess of bones for your trouble. Just can't be good to some folks. Furnish em water all year and you want somethin done and it don't work two ways. . . ."

This was more than Sam could take. He had been told about that well water once too often.

He went out where Henry was standing.

"God damn you," Sam said, "I've got a bellyful of your way of actin. No matter what I do, or how hard I try to get along with you, you act like it ain't fair. Now get this straight: we don't want no more of your God damned well water. We'll drink out of the river like cattle and hogs. If we catch typhoid, we catch it. But I've taken the last thing off of you I'm ever gonna take. You come over here one more time feelin sorry for yourself and cusin me o not doin right, and I'm gonna beat your God damned eyes out."

Henry turned and walked twenty yards away. At this distance he faced Sam and said, "We'll see whether you can treat me like this and get away with it. We'll see if maybe you don't get sorry you talked to me like that."

Then he was gone.

Sam went back in the house, feeling bad. You always felt bad after seeing Henry.

That night Henry's cows ate absolutely all of Sam's garden. Pigs rooted up the tiny potatoes and carrots that were underground. But at daylight only their tracks were there. The stock had been returned to its pens.

When the family stood with Sam at the back door next morning seeing this devastation, Sam said what he had often said before, "Try not to fret. We'll make out."

Daisy did not come to breakfast. When they heard her under the house, Sam said, "Don't disturb her. We'll each bear this in our own way."

This was Thursday. On Wednesday Sam had seen Henry bait his buffalo hole with corn. He knew Henry would go there Sunday morning to fish. That would be time enough. Henry would be off his own farm, which, Sam seemed to remember, was an important legal point.

26

WHEN Sam awoke on Sunday morning he could see through the cracks in the wall that the sky was a clear, vibrant blue. He did not want any breakfast, but, to appear relaxed and normal, he ate his bread and drank his coffee. When he had finished, he said, "I got a trot line set out down at the river. I'm goin down there."

The children wanted to go with him.

"No, you kids stay and help Mamma," he said. "This afternoon, maybe."

As he left the house Nona followed him outside.

"I know what you're gonna do," she said, "and I don't care."

He approached the creek in a roundabout way. He

wanted Henry still to be there. But as he walked, Sam
somehow felt like a stranger to himself, that he was going
to do a thing which was not to his taste and not of his
choice, something he had so long avoided, but toward
which circumstance had continued to push him, each
time, a little harder.

He was going to the river and thrash Henry Devers till
he screamed, and after. But without hate, in despair and
loneliness and utter dejection. He was going to follow
out a pattern that had no meaning to him. He was going
to do it now when it was too late, because he knew nothing else to do.

But as he passed his trot line he saw it moving slowly,
up and down. Only a powerful force could have pulled
it so evenly. Totally without joy, he knew he had caught
Lead Pencil, and the emptiness of this great feat, the desolation of this hour, when he should have been exultant,
squeezed his heart like a strong hand gripping.

Mechanically he performed what should have been the
highest adventure of his life. A few minutes later the big
fish was tethered by the boat rope to a thick willow sapling that would bend but never break.

That done, Sam went on down the river.

As he appeared quietly beside Henry, Henry jumped.

"Gee!" Henry said nervously. "You scared me, Sam.
I didn't hear nobody."

"Didn't you?"

"They ain't bitin good this mornin."

"What have you got to say, Henry?"

"About what?"

"Your stock."

Henry's tone changed abruptly.

"I'm tired of your naggin and whinin, Sam Tucker."

"I never came to nag and whine. I came here to whip you, Henry."

This seemed to release a spring in Henry that had been quietly winding tighter and tighter.

From the newspaper beside him he snatched a butcher knife. Sunlight danced on the tiny scars in its blade where it had just been sharpened on a coarse stone. Without a word, his face blue-white with the hate of fear, he ran at Sam, who scrambled up the bank, straight through a tangle of brier vines.

Henry was fast. Through the openings Sam was making in the vines, Henry was drawing closer.

Sam felt something hot rip across his back. The touch of the blade filled him with terror.

At the same time his right eye saw a four-foot length of green elm limb lying in the weeds just ahead. And the urgency of what he now must do, the complete concentration necessary to doing it, thrust terror out of his mind. Swooping, at full speed, his hand shot out toward the limb. Sam knew that if he lost his footing Henry would slash him to pieces with the butcher knife, that he was taking a desperate chance. Yet it was his only hope, and with the certainty of absolute desperation, his whole being keyed to the highest, most brittle stage of efficiency, he was taking that chance.

His hand touched the elm club, clutched it, and dragged

it through the air behind his body. Now it was grasped firmly in both hands. He got ready to swing.

Then he saw that Henry had caught his leg in a vine and fallen on the ground, ten feet back. He was on all fours, pulling the knife blade out of the ground.

Quickly Sam moved in.

Henry was fixed with horror, unable to move. His hand went limp. The butcher knife fell to the ground.

"Please, Sam. I got a family. They need me to work. My kids would starve."

He shut his eyes tightly, covered his face with one arm, the back of his head with the other.

"Please. Oh, God, please! I don't want to die. I don't want to be hammered to pieces with no club."

As Sam came within clubbing range, Henry was whimpering in gasps like a badly hurt dog.

Sam picked up the butcher knife and threw it in the river.

"Get up, Henry," he said. "Now walk out in the middle of that open field."

When they got there, Sam made Henry hand over his pocket knife, then threw it and the club away.

"Henry," he said, "I've tried every peaceable way I know of to get along with you. It hasn't worked. Now I'm goin to whip you. You've been dirtyin me up, you son of a bitch, ever since I came here. You been buildin up a meanness in me all that time and now I'm gonna turn it loose on you."

The running, the blood dripping down Sam's back, had

done something to him. His hot body was eager to get at Henry.

Cat-quick, Henry struck out. His fist caught Sam on the cheek bone. Sam's knees buckled. But they didn't go down, and his long left arm reached through that rain of fists and fastened on Henry's shirt front. Sam's heels dug into the ground. And it began. Sam remembered only the devastated garden; the sound of Daisy's muffled sobs coming from beneath the house; that Henry had tried, and succeeded in, wrecking his desperate struggle to feed his family, to live, to exist beside the river. . . .

Suddenly it dawned on Sam that Henry, whom he had just given a stout kick, was lying motionless on the ground. He looked more like a dead thing than an unconscious man. Sam didn't much care if he was. Nothing mattered any more, since Daisy would not get her ribbon. That was the thing that . . . He couldn't bear to think of it any longer.

He dragged Henry to the river and stretched him on the bank. It was five or ten minutes before he even began to groan. By then Sam had become a little more calm.

At first Henry only lay there and moaned. Then, beneath his battered, half-closed lids, he began to take intensely eager and curious glances around him, as if he were trying to convince himself that he was still alive. When he saw Sam sitting beside him, he closed his eyes again quickly.

"I reckon you'll live over it, all right," Sam said.

Henry groaned pitifully.

"I got somethin to say to you, Henry, if you've got your wits together."

Again Henry only groaned.

"We done had our little spat," Sam said. "Seems like there wasn't any way to get around it. But that's all over now. For my part, there's no hard feelins left over. I ain't goin to crow about lickin you. Ain't gonna tell a soul. But there's somethin I want to ask you."

"What?" Henry said, some of the normal sharpness having returned to his eyes.

"You turned your stock in on my garden. They ruined it and I ain't demandin damages."

"I guess not," Henry said. "You done done em."

"What I mean is, you got that great big garden over there, and your neighbor's got his tail in a crack. You saw the shape my little boy got in this spring. Well, you've fixed it so he'll be in it again. I know no man would be that mean on purpose after stoppin to think. No man would want to break my little girl's heart by snatchin that cannin ribbon out of her hands. You was mad when you done it, but you've had time to cool off by now. And you got that big ole garden at your place, and most of it'll just stand there and rot and go to seed. Looks like any human would say, 'Go on over there, Sam, and get what you need. There's a big plenty for both of us.' "

Henry had his answer ready.

"I would," he said, "if we could spare it. I planted a garden that size because we needed that much stuff our ownselfs."

Sam could see it was hopeless. To break the spell of

jelled futility, he said, "Get up. Let's go. You got some places on your head needs doctorin."

At the sapling Sam pulled his fish out of the water.

"Jesus Christ!" Henry said. "That's the biggest fish I ever saw. If he won't go sixty pounds, he won't weigh nothin."

"I figgered sixty-five."

A strange nervousness was beginning to possess Henry. "When'd you catch im?"

"Smornin. On my way to you."

"Sam."

"What?"

"I been tryin to catch me a big fish all my life."

"So's a lot of folks."

"Well, I just been figgerin. I'd take your sworn word for anything."

"Sure nuff?"

"Look, Sam. Let's do this. You give me that fish and swear never to tell you caught it. If you'll do that, you can get anything you want out of my garden. You can have it all."

For a moment Sam stood there.

If he kept the fish and sold it in town, it was too big, the meat too coarse, to bring more than a nickel a pound: three dollars at the most. And that would not buy enough vegetables. But the honor, the distinction, of catching it would remain his own. This fish meant that his name, in conjunction with Lead Pencil's, would become a legend and would live when he was dead. It was the climax of his lifelong association with the river and would never come again. It was his claim to a kind of immortality that meant something to him. It would make him a big man in the eyes of anybody who had ever fished in the San Pedro.

He thought of the blue ribbon on Daisy's breast. Probably there would be printing on it in gold, like ribbons at the Hackberry poultry show. He remembered the wrinkled, dusty-purple spots on Jot's body.

He was going to let Henry have the fish, all right. But for a moment longer Sam held the rope, looking at Henry, trying to figure what real good it would ever do him to be able to pretend he'd caught Lead Pencil. And as Sam stood there, he supposed there must be two kinds of people: those who want to be, and those others who are satisfied simply to appear to be, whatever thing it is their hearts long for.

Never in their association had Henry been so genuinely pathetic to Sam, so futilely groping. Never before had Sam so clearly realized that Henry was willing to try to hide from his own lostness behind a set of appearances which he himself knew were false. It was if Henry's conscience and the measure of his success were situated only in the minds of others, as if he had despaired of ever finding strength and confidence and peace of mind except as a reflection of other men's approbation.

And Sam was ashamed to have looked upon this pitiable thing in its moment of utter nakedness.

He held out the fish.

That afternoon, like locusts, or even the Deverses' cows, Sam and his family began at one end of Henry Devers's garden and came out the other. They could hear Henry in the house trying to quiet his wife.

Since the materials with which they were working were perishable, Sam and Nona washed and peeled and cooked and canned throughout the night. When Daisy awoke, one hundred-odd jars had been filled. Nona fed the children and sent Daisy to school, then rejoined Sam at the stove.

At noon Daisy ran away from school and caught a ride home to show her ribbon. Then, to make a great day complete, one of the Deverses' children brought them a small mess of catfish.

After supper that night, the whole family sat around the fireplace in genuine contentment, their minds full of the canned vegetables which the children's schooling had brought them.

The lamp, beside which Daisy sat on sleepy exhibition, shone strongly on the blue-and-gold ribbon.

Unimpressed by this hour of glory, Jot and Zoonie played happily on the floor.

In her chair, Nona slept.

Before going to bed, Sam made a cigarette and went out and sat on the steps. He looked at the sky and saw a flock of ducks fly over. Soon wild fowl would be stopping on the river. There were two old twelve-gauge shotgun shells lying around the house somewhere which he would use if he could borrow a gun.

His play-pretty year was ended.

He threw his cigarette into the yard and went in the house and woke Nona.

"Better get to bed, Honey," he said. "There's always another day."

She smiled, exhausted.

"I'm tard," she said. "Almost too tard to move."

Her eyes fell on the sea of preserved food, the ribbon.

"But it don't differ," she said, "long as we're gettin somewhere."

Granny, who had already retired, raised herself on one elbow and gave them a glare.

"Some folks," she said impatiently, "is tryin to sleep," and flounced back onto her pillow.

AFTERWORD

By the time of his death in 1956, George Sessions Perry had moved far from his Texas origins and gained success and recognition as a reporter and feature writer that for a time overshadowed his earlier achievements in fiction. Ultimately, however, Perry's reputation as a writer will rest on the picture of rural Texas that he created in his fiction, most notably *Hold Autumn in Your Hand,* published in 1941. This novel, which won the annual award of the Texas Institute of Letters in 1941 and the National Book Award in 1942, was preceded by a lighthearted, slightly bawdy novel, *Walls Rise Up,* a chronicle of the adventures of three picaro-type characters who spend a summer living underneath a bridge on the Brazos River. In 1944 Perry followed these two works with *Hackberry Cavalier,* a collection of seventeen short stories that feature indigent but entertaining poor whites from the backwoods and small towns of East Texas. After a stint as a war correspondent in World War II, Perry completed his writings about Texas with three nonfiction books: *Texas: A World in Itself,* a lively account of Texas history, culture, and traditions; *My Granny Van,* an affectionate portrait of Perry's astonishing and irascible grandmother, who was the terror of Rockdale, Texas; and *Tale of a Foolish*

Farmer, an account of Perry's own emotionally rewarding but financially disastrous venture into farming on the tract of land that had been the setting for *Hold Autumn in Your Hand.*

Although Perry traveled widely when he was writing feature articles for the *Country Gentleman* and *The Saturday Evening Post* and in the later years of his life maintained a home in Guilford, Connecticut, his artistic consciousness was formed and largely remained in Rockdale, Texas, where he was born in 1910. As the son of a pharmacist, he lived in town and was not directly involved in farming or ranching, yet all his early writing reveals an intense awareness of the problems of those who make their living from the land: rain, drought, insects, blight, and the price of cotton and cattle. This concern developed in those formative years from 1925 to 1935 when Perry saw great changes take place in the agricultural area of which Rockdale was the center. In less than ten years the price of cotton went from fifty cents a pound to five cents a pound; what had once been rich land was exhausted because it had been mined for high profits; what had once been a prosperous community was hit by a depression, both local and national. And at the very bottom of the social and economic structure were the sharecroppers and the tenant farmers, now virtually destitute.

Perry's conscience was troubled because he, as a middle-class town man with a small private income, was not actually affected by the disaster around him. He tried to expunge his guilt and pity by expressing in writing his anger at a society that simply accepted rural poverty as a way of life. From 1931 to 1937 he wrote six novels and more than fifty short stories, nearly all of them in the tradition of the protest fiction of the 1930s and many of them focusing on the kind of feudalistic system in which Sam Tucker is caught in *Hold Autumn in Your Hand.* In one book he wrote:

> Farmers are slaves, serfs. . . . There is no use talking about the law. . . . Everybody is entirely within his rights. They are all just sitting there in the protecting arms of the law waiting for you to come and bleed yourself to death in their buckets.

If Perry found the townspeople callous, he found publishers indifferent and unwilling to upset the public with tales of poverty. Nevertheless, he went on writing his chronicles of small-town and rural Texas and accumulating a stack of rejected manuscripts. Those six years of apparently unrewarded labor were far from fruitless. For one thing, Perry collected a storehouse of anecdotes, characters, and situations which he used in his later work, and he developed his talent for reproducing the idioms and speech patterns that give authenticity to his stories of Texas poor whites. He also seems to have written much of the bitterness out of his system and let his affection for the land and his delight in people come to the surface. His first comic story about a backwoods Texan was accepted in 1937, and by the time he wrote *Hold Autumn in Your Hand* in 1940 he was able to tell his story of a tenant farmer with humor as well as compassion. By then he had also realized that although the very poor may be victims, they can also be people of dignity and courage and sensitivity.

Hold Autumn in Your Hand was Perry's favorite among his works, perhaps because it most clearly expressed his beliefs, his affections, and his concerns. It reflects his deep affinity for nature, his feeling that hunting and fishing are a kind of religious activity that renew a man's spirit; thus when Sam Tucker is in the woods or on the river, he becomes a superbly competent primitive whose finely honed instincts give him dominance over his immediate world. Perry also sees farming as an occupation which, however risky, is basically good because it fills man's primitive need to create, and again and again he uses sexual imagery to describe Sam's relationship with the land. He actually feels a sensuous love for his crop and wants to "hold autumn in his hand." Perry's love of the river and the woods and of the rich bottomland beside them is matched by his deep affection for the people of the region. Most of them are poor and uneducated, and to an outsider their lives would seem stark and meaningless. Perry, however, finds them attractive;

he respects their peasant strength, their ability to endure, their natural good manners, and their willingness to help each other.

Sam Tucker's life centers on the basic needs: work and food. To emphasize this truth, Perry constructs *Hold Autumn in Your Hand* around a series of incidents that follow the rhythm of the growing cycle: plowing, planting, cultivating, and harvesting. The events of the novel begin in the winter when the land is fallow and move steadily toward that focal point in every farmer's life, fall. The harvest, good or bad, is the climax of the year, and Perry also makes it the climax of the book. Woven into the story of tilling the land are accounts of Sam's other activities, and they too follow the pattern of the seasons: hunting in the winter, fishing in the spring, berry picking and honey gathering in the summer, and syrup making in the fall. Even the leisure activities revolve around food. In fact, almost everything Sam does in the book is basic, and his life is not appreciably different from what it would have been if he had lived a hundred years ago. The ironic difference is that then he would have been a successful man because his skills and highly developed instincts fit him for a frontier society; in his own time, he is a failure in an industrialist and capitalistic society.

Because Perry depicts Sam Tucker as a vigorous and optimistic man who not only copes with day-to-day crises but really enjoys life and makes the most of it, the casual reader of *Hold Autumn in Your Hand* may not fully realize that the implications of the book are gloomy, and that it is implicit throughout the book that Sam must leave the land if he and his family are to survive. In Perry's original ending for the book, Sam himself realized that his "play pretty" year of living by the river and pitting himself against the backland had been a sensuous self-indulgence, not a useful or practical thing to do. In that version of the book Sam comes to the conclusion that he must go to Houston and find work in a factory. Fully aware of what the change will mean to him, Sam muses:

> He had had his year. It had been hard, but exquisitely rewarding in that he had been able to employ the multitude of old skills and understandings that his past, his sand-hill heritage, had stored up for him. . . . Now he must look straightforwardly into the future. Daisy and Jot could not be raised as urchins. Nona had endured too much already. Next week he would start the long journey to Houston where the mills and factories were, where a man could earn two and three, perhaps four dollars a day. It was the only way in which a man with no education, no capital of land or money, could any longer support his family in anything but squalor.
>
>   . . . He could no longer find refuge in the

land except as an admission of weakness and
loneliness. He could no longer justify his desire
to do the best for the family with his clinging
to the land. . . . If amid the stink and clangor
of the factory, there was no comfort for the
spirit, then the spirit must do without. The
play pretty year, the last echo of childhood in
which one is protected by the known and no
defeat can be final, was over.

This original ending appeared in the first three
drafts of the novel, but the published version ends
with Sam and Nona in triumph over having canned
enough food for the winter; there is simply no
mention of the future. The reason for the change is
summarized succinctly in a note Mrs. Perry at-
tached to the typescript of the third draft of the
book. It says:

This manuscript . . . has the original ending
wherein Sam realized that the only way he
could make a living for his family was by
giving up farming and going to Houston to
work in a factory. The editors at Viking
convinced GSP that the book would be more
effective if it ended on a more victorious note
for Sam, leaving him on the land which he
loved.

In spite of the revised ending, *Hold Autumn in Your
Hand* remains a realistic and graphic account of the
life of a southern tenant farmer during the depres-

sion of the thirties. But it is more than a regional
novel or an example of a particular school of
American fiction. It is also a moving statement of a
timeless theme, man's struggle to tame the land,
and it is a powerful statement of one of the ways in
which the American dream has failed.

For Perry, his novel about Sam Tucker remained
the peak of his literary career. Between the time he
finished the book and the time he became a war
correspondent, he began work on another novel and
wrote several short stories, mostly humorous ones,
but he was never again able to produce a long work
of serious fiction. The war itself marked a watershed
in Perry's life and his career. Perry had signed on as
a war correspondent partly out of a sense of guilt
because he had been declared medically unfit for
the service, but he found himself in the middle of
combat in the Sicily invasion. His wife and friends
say that he was never able to forget the nightmare
of agony and fear he went through in the harbor
and on the beaches at Salerno. The truths he saw
during the war seemed more than he could face—he
couldn't write fiction about them and he could not
write fiction without talking about them. To avoid
the issue he turned to writing feature articles and
soon was making both money and a national
reputation for himself.

In the late 1940s Perry decided to use the money
he was making in journalism to disprove the adage
"You can't go home again." He bought the river-

bottom farm that had been the site of *Hold Autumn in Your Hand.* As he wrote in *Tale of a Foolish Farmer,*

> I envied Sam Tucker . . . his almost godlike sense of creation as he watched his labors materialize into substantial fruit and beauty out of the earth. Worse yet, I began to flirt with the notion—then actually become wedded to it—that I, a townbred man, could do the job better in practice than, in the loving arms of my imagination, Sam had done. There may even have been a touch of the Quixotic notion that I . . . should undergo the same rigors as my protagonist.

Perry bought the farm, built a house on it, fenced it, and stocked it with registered Hereford cattle. It became his play pretty, but one that he could not afford to depend on any more than Sam could. In order to support his love affair with the land, he had to travel urban America writing, ironically, a very profitable series of *Post* articles called "Cities of America."

During those postwar years many of Perry's unpublished writings reflected a growing sense of guilt about having abandoned fiction for the more lucrative and surer returns of journalism. Probably that guilt contributed partially to his increasingly heavy drinking, but he was also drinking more and more to combat the chronic pain from worsening arthritis of the spine. By 1950, he also showed concrete signs of mental illness. For the last five years before he died in 1956, Perry was caught in a three-dimensional nightmare of alcoholism, arthritis, and mental illness. One affected the other, and, separately and together, they made his life a living hell. A huge man, he was almost unable to move and, toward the end, also unable to work. In the last years the *Hold Autumn* farm had to be sold to pay hospital and living expenses—the tragedy had indeed come full cycle. At last, driven by phantom voices which harangued him constantly about his guilt, Perry walked into the river near his Connecticut home. When his body was found two months later, the coroner's verdict was accidental death by drowning.

Maxine C. Hairston
University of Texas at Austin
Austin, Texas